SOLO
PASS

ALSO BY RONALD DE FEO

Calling Mr. King

OTHER PRESS ■ NEW YORK

SOLO PASS

PASS

RONALD DE FEO

Copyright © 2013 Ronald De Feo

An earlier version of this narration first appeared in
a shorter form in *The Hudson Review*.

Production Editor: Yvonne E. Cárdenas
Text Designer: Chris Welch
This book was set in 12 pt Granjon by Alpha Design & Composition
of Pittsfield, NH

10 9 8 7 6 5 4 3 2 1

LIBRARY OF CONGRESS CATALOGING-IN-PUBLICATION DATA

De Feo, Ronald.
  Solo pass / Ronald De Feo.
    p. cm.
  ISBN 978-1-59051-586-0 (trade pbk. : acid-free paper) —
ISBN 978-1-59051-581-5 (eBook)   1. Mentally ill—Fiction.
2. Leave of absence—Fiction.   3. Psychic trauma—Fiction.
4. Homecoming—Fiction.   5. Psychological fiction.   I. Title.
  PS3604.E1226S65 2013
  813'.6—dc23

                                                2012013155

PART I

THOUGHT THAT I looked ready now, so I asked for a solo pass.

To my surprise, they agreed. Tomorrow would be the day.

It began to feel like an event. Which was understandable. Because I hadn't been outside by myself in nearly two months. It could just as well have been two years.

I had asked twice before, but the doctors had said no, claiming that I wasn't quite ready. Now I suppose they considered me ready enough, though in some ways I felt much the same as I did when I wasn't, except for a tinge of calmness and control that had come over me unexpectedly, strangely, in recent days. The old feelings were still there, the old thoughts and fears, the anger, but more often than not I was able to ignore them or at least stop them before they got out of hand.

I DIDN'T PUSH things. Some patients when they're ready for a solo pass ask for a whole day on the outside. But I told Dr. Petersen, who's been following my case ever since I arrived at Essex and was sent up to the mental ward, that I'd leave after lunch and be back around six, just in time for supper. Fine, she said, no problem, make a good half day of it. You could tell that she was impressed by such a conservative, mature plan.

Yes, I've learned to understand their thinking and how to impress them, which according to my roommate Carl is the first big step toward getting out of here for good. Carl should know. He goes mad periodically and has been in and out of this place as well as in and out of other mental wards and hospitals throughout the city. He thinks of them as specialized hotels. "And this is one of the best," he said. "Nice rooms, wall-to-wall carpeting, decent food. I give it four stars." As he sees it, there's only one problem: it's easy to check in, but not so easy to check out.

Carl used to be the manager of the appliance department of a big department store. At work he would wear a white carnation in his lapel, the mark of an executive. There isn't anything he doesn't know about refrigerators or washers and dryers. Ask him about toasters and microwave ovens and he can go on for hours. Once I told him that the inside of my metal coffeepot at home was so stained and corroded that it had a lethal look about it, that you drank its contents at your own risk, and that I really had to invest in a new one. Well, he must have rattled off a dozen or so brands, describing both the regular sort of pot and the kind you plug in, citing the positives and negatives, the features and capacity of each. I was very impressed. Too bad that depression often gets the better of him, a kind of visiting darkness and despair he simply doesn't understand and doesn't have the power to evict. The crisis came one day when he was demonstrating a food processor to a customer and began, for no particular reason, to weep. He couldn't stop weeping, sank down to the floor, and was eventually carried off by two security people. They tried to calm him, but soon realized that it was hopeless and called for an ambulance. That was five years ago. He's been in and out of work, and in and out of hospitals, ever since.

I suppose there's no good explanation for why one mind suddenly goes off while another holds firm. Apparently some minds are weaker than others, more sensitive and breakable. And I suppose it's best that they are in the minority or else the streets would be filled with lunatics.

Although I was concerned about going out, I wasn't as concerned as I might have been. After all, I'd been out a few times before on a group pass, where you join other patients and are led by nurses or aides and can walk only a few blocks from the hospital. No one on staff is in uniform and no patient is in hospital dress, but people on the street usually realize that this group is pretty peculiar. Particularly when some patients are heavily medicated and walk about fuzzy-brained and half alive or wear odd combinations of clothes, like Mrs. Clark, who went out one day with rainbow-colored stockings, a plaid skirt, a striped blouse, and a fur piece made from some diseased animal killed out of mercy. Or when a patient is too free and loud, like big Wally Weston, who'd comment on wonders passing by. "A PUPPY!" he'd yell upon seeing any small dog. Or "I'd like her to be the mother of my child!" upon seeing any attractive woman. I sometimes talk with Wally in the dayroom, enjoy his childlike ways and silly stories, but I learned to keep away from him on group walks.

In fact, I tried to keep my distance from the group in general while still being a part of it. I walked alertly, commandingly, as if I were an aide and responsible for this sorry collection of souls. I think I fooled a lot of people. Once when we were waiting at the corner for the light to change and I was standing at the rear of the group, a man on the street began talking to me. "I don't envy you," he said, "having a job like this. Must get to you every now and then." "Oh, I'm used to it by now," I said. "They retarded or what?" "Psych ward," I said. "No kiddin'? What's that like?" "Crazy," I said.

Any concern I now had about going out came from the new situation—there wouldn't be anyone with me this time. I'd be completely alone.

Funny. When I was with the group, I wanted to stay away from it. The patients humiliated me by their presence, their obvious sickness. But now I wondered how I would do without them, particularly if I started to feel shaky, to sense all of the space and emptiness around me, with no one to cling to if I found myself growing weak, losing control.

Dr. Petersen told me about the solo pass in the late morning. Called me into the office she usually uses for therapy sessions to report that they had all agreed to grant me a solo. By *all* I mean the doctors on the ward, including Mortonberg, the head of the unit, and the nurses, who are really around the patients most, like parents caring for infants. Odd when you think about it. All those eyes had been on me, looking for positive behavior, signs of adjustment.

"So how are you feeling about this?" Dr. Petersen asked."Going out on your own tomorrow."

"I'm delighted," I said. "Absolutely delighted."

Dr. Petersen smiled widely as if I'd said something funny. Or perhaps peculiar. I couldn't quite judge, but either way her reaction disturbed me.

"Did I say something wrong?" I asked, in a tone that was perhaps too harsh. So I then smiled to indicate that all was well and friendly. I've learned that they don't appreciate anger. Particularly when you're in line for a solo pass.

"Oh, no," she said, "it's just the way you put it. *I'm delighted.* It's not the sort of expression we usually hear. I can't remember a patient ever saying that he was *delighted* about anything. It sounds very formal, like something from another age."

I quickly explained that I was a great reader of old British writers, particularly of Dickens, also of Trollope and a bit of Galsworthy, and such language had probably stuck in my brain. "I suppose I'm something of an Anglophile. Went to England once, with my ex-wife. London began to feel like home. More like home than this city, actually. Sometimes—"

I stopped myself. I was rambling on for no good reason—which could be interpreted as a sign of a brain still in disarray. "Excuse me," I said, knowingly, "I'm straying."

As I sat there face-to-face with Dr. Petersen, I began to wonder why I should fear her even a little. Of course, her opinion of me, of my progress, or lack of it, could affect the length of my stay. But physically speaking there was, and still is, nothing fearful about her. She's of average height—quite a bit shorter than me in fact. Trim enough to be regarded as skinny. Has short black hair and a vaguely pleasant face, though it's too long and thin like the rest of her. And her somewhat pointy, bumpy nose sometimes recalls a carrot. All said, she isn't particularly attractive, but as far as psychiatrists go, who tend to be a queer, funny-looking lot, she's not half bad. Her best feature is her legs, which during this little meeting I couldn't help but notice. I saw them as very long and shapely, almost like those of a model. It was odd to think of my doctor as being so exposed and resembling such a type. Somehow it took away from the seriousness of her profession, reduced her authority.

And now that I was looking at her in a new way—perhaps because I was soon to be free of her and the hospital, at least for half a day—I began to resent such a person serving as my caretaker and judge. Because she was really nothing special at all. And worse, she was several years younger than me—somewhere in her early thirties.

"So," she said, "have you decided what you'll do, where you'll go?"

"I thought I might take a bus."

"Uh-huh."

"Go for a ride."

"I see."

"It feels so long since I've traveled anywhere."

"Any particular destination?"

"No. I'll just ride around and then get off when it feels right."

I could tell that she wanted more details, a little more certainty on my part. So I said that I'd probably head east, since it was more elegant on that side of town. And I certainly could use some elegance at this point in my life. Besides, the area around the hospital was old and ugly, with its warehouses and garages and auto supply shops, and I had seen enough of it from the hospital windows and on group walks.

"Well, that's understandable," she remarked. "But no one expects you to stay in this neighborhood. In fact, I think it's a good thing that you don't want to keep close, that you're willing to leave us behind for a while."

Tomorrow is only the beginning, I wanted to tell her. Soon I won't have to worry at all about what you think of me or my behavior. I'll be permanently free. And you, along with this place, will disappear.

Too bad that I can't rid myself of all doctors so easily. Prodski has long been out of sight and out of my life and by now should have faded away to nothing. But unfortunately he has taken up residence in my brain.

I mentioned him to Dr. Petersen when I first arrived here, though I don't remember saying much about the business. A passing reference was all. I believed I described him as a "rotten scoundrel" and an "uncouth bastard." Prodski was the therapist I was seeing when I first began feeling even stranger than usual. And I finally stopped seeing him when I lost my job and could no longer afford his fee.

I don't think Dr. Petersen took my comments very seriously because my brain was badly muddled at the time and I was probably talking a lot of nonsense. Later on, when I was settled on the ward and my head was a little clearer, I was tempted to tell her all about the man, his betrayal, my loathing, but Mandy Reed, who, like Carl, is a very experienced patient, though just a kid by comparison, urged me not to say a thing. "Don't be too honest with these creeps," she said, meaning the staff, "particularly when it comes to one of their own. They'll only hold it against you. Just tell them what they want to hear. Stay nice and calm. Pretend you're fine. Talk about the future, and all that crap. And whatever you do, don't say that you feel like killing somebody. They'll ship you off to Courtland and throw away the key."

Courtland is the state hospital where the ward doctors send you if your brain fails to straighten itself out in a reasonable amount of time. After all, Essex is a medical hospital with only two mental wards, this one, for your standard case, and the one upstairs, for your violent sort. The wards can hold only so many patients and eventually have to make room for new breakdowns. When Mandy had a really bad spell a few years back that neither she nor her medication could shake she was sent from some downtown hospital to Courtland and kept there for months. "And if you think the patients here are bad," she told me, "you should see the collection in Courtland—a bunch of frigging zombies talking to walls and chairs."

There had been times during my stay here when I feared that just being around disturbed people would make me sicker than I already was and that I might very well end up in Courtland or some similar asylum for the rest of my life. I still have that fear, but to a much lesser degree. Because I believe that I'm much stronger now and much less impressionable. And, even more important, I now appear to others—experts in such matters—as someone who is approaching normality.

"Any of those strange feelings lately?" Dr. Petersen asked, referring to the feelings that used to creep up on me—at my job, at home with my ex-wife, just about anywhere and at any time. There I'd be by the window of my office staring out at the office buildings across the way or sunk down in my favorite easy chair at home studying Elizabeth reading on the sofa, and I'd suddenly feel that I didn't belong, that I had been placed in someone else's life, that everyone and everything around me was foreign, unfamiliar, wrong.

No, I told her. None at all. And I smiled again, this time to indicate that I now regarded those feelings as rather ridiculous, a product of an illness that was no longer with me. Why, the very mention of them amused me more than anything else. I conveyed this amusement well. Yes, I believe I was very convincing.

"Hear any voices lately?" she asked, though I couldn't recall ever having complained of voices. This was Mandy Reed's problem, not mine.

"Only from the CD player in the dayroom."

The joke put her at ease, which was my intention.

"Especially Bonnie Tyler's voice, " I added.

"Who?"

"Bonnie Tyler. I guess you'd call her a pop singer. With a big raspy voice. Don't know whatever happened to her. She had a big hit years ago—'Total Eclipse of the Heart.' It's ridiculous, but it sort of gets to you."

"And this song is a favorite of yours?" Dr. Petersen was obviously unable to relate me to such music.

"Oh, no, it's not my choice. Wally likes to play it. Wally Weston. Can't get enough of it at times. He says that he wants Bonnie Tyler to become his wife. He says that he would never break her heart like the man in the song."

"I don't think I've ever heard it," said Dr. Petersen. "I'm afraid I'm limited to the classics."

"So was I—before I was committed."

We chatted on, just like old friends, though I very much watched my step, carefully choosing my words, only pretending to relax my guard.

"So you're going to the East Side tomorrow. But you live on the West Side. Any plans to visit your apartment?"

The question confused me for a moment. I had gotten the impression during our sessions together that Dr. Petersen was against my returning home too soon, even for a visit, felt that I should stay for a while with my uncle Arthur, my closest relative—in fact, the only one left in the city, and one of the few relatives still alive in this world in general. Why ask for trouble was what she seemed to be saying. My apartment had been a place of sadness, of sickness. The sunless rooms had darkened my spirit. My only company had been the television, the radio, the voices in the walls. And then one day, I just couldn't stand it all any longer.

I decided to give her a balanced plan, one that was neither too cautious nor too reckless, showing how aware I was of my limitations and also of my responsibilities. "I suppose I *should* stop by my place," I said, "just to see if everything is in order. Though my uncle has a key and has been checking the apartment every few days."

"Yes, I know. He told me."

"You spoke to my uncle?" I was surprised because nei- ther Uncle Arthur nor Dr. Petersen had mentioned the fact. Despite their good intentions, I don't think I appreci- ated their talking behind my back.

"Just in the hall once or twice. I noticed him visiting with you in the dayroom. Seems like a very nice man."

"Yes, " I said cautiously, not sure where she was going with this business, or if she was going anywhere at all, "he's a good old salt."

She looked amused again. "You do come out with the oddest expressions."

"Sorry," I said. I was about to blame English literature again.

"Your uncle seems very concerned about you."

"He's always been my favorite relative. And he likes to take care of people. He took care of my aunt Helen for years. She had some kind of fatal disease. When she died, he had no one to take care of anymore, so he concentrated on other sick people. It's a good thing that he has a lot of friends who are old and sick. Otherwise he wouldn't know what to do with himself."

"I understand that he even helped clean up your apart- ment after you were admitted."

"That's what he told me. He told me that everything is fine now, all neat and tidy. He said that he had to throw out some things, things that couldn't be repaired."

"You mean the things that you broke—broke purposely."

"All of that is still vague in my head. I know that it happened, but I still find it hard to believe. It's more like another person did it—somebody like me, but not really me."

I was suddenly worried that I had offered a bit too much information, and it had been weird information besides. These doctors press you to open up, but the more you do the more you leave yourself open to more questions and attacks. The trick is to be chatty yet discreet.

"As we've discussed," said Dr. Petersen, "we sometimes block out unpleasant memories. Does it still bother you that you can't remember that day?"

I thought carefully this time before answering.

"No," I finally said. "Because if I did act a certain way once, I don't anymore. So what's the point in trying to remember?"

She seemed to like this answer, smiling softly in approval. "Well," she said, "that's certainly one way to look at it."

Actually it troubled me that the day of my breakdown was something of a blur in my mind. At times I'd concentrate hard and try to bring certain incidents into focus—the authorities arriving at my door, the trip to the hospital, the arrival at the emergency room—but they remained vague, lacking detail, substance. I'd grow frustrated and then angry by my inability to clearly recall this day. I'd strain my brain to form a scene and then put myself in it. But even if I was able to imagine myself, say, in the emergency room being examined, having a light flashed in my eyes, the experience had almost no reality, and as such meant nothing, led to nothing.

I wanted to talk to her about medication, but thought that the question would make me seem weak and unsure of myself. My concern, though, was valid since I was now off heavy-duty drugs and taking only one pill three times a day. This seemed okay for now, here on the ward, but I wondered if ten milligrams would be enough to hold me for a full afternoon solo.

"So," she said, "you're going over to the East Side tomorrow. Because you like the neighborhood."

"Yes, it makes me feel good."

"Do you have a special place in mind? A favorite store perhaps?"

They still don't trust me, I thought, trying not to let my irritation show. They want to give me a day's freedom, but still feel the need to guide me, control me.

"A bookshop," I said, and was proud of myself for coming up with a legitimate answer so quickly. "In fact, there are a few bookshops on my list." I had, of course, no such list, but it sounded impressive to say that I had.

"That's fine. I think it's good to have a specific place in mind and a place that you enjoy. It should make things a little less stressful, and more pleasurable."

"Less like a test, you mean."

"I wouldn't really put it that way. But do you look at this as a test? Is that the way you see it?"

Just then someone knocked on the door. Saved by the knock, I thought, because I was beginning to feel that Dr. Petersen was trying to trip me up. Perhaps she was having second thoughts about my solo.

Luckily for me, the knock wasn't just a quick interruption. It was made by Nurse Jackson, who told Dr. Petersen that she was wanted upstairs on the violent ward. So she had to excuse herself, reminding me that she would have to sign my solo pass tomorrow before I left.

"Thanks, Virginia," I said to her as she walked down the hall.

She stopped in her tracks and turned. "What did you say?"

"I said, Thanks."

"Not that. You said my name. You called me by my first name."

"Did I?"

"You called me Virginia."

"Sorry, I didn't even realize it. Must have been a slip." But I had done it purposely. As someone who was about to be released for a day, I suppose I was feeling bold and wanted to remind her that we were really equals and as such could dispense with formalities and titles.

"We'll have to discuss this later," she said, her face somewhat flushed, as Millie Jackson unlocked the ward door and held it open for her.

What was there to discuss? I wondered.

I returned to my room, feeling quite pleased with myself for having unsettled her, this woman, this doctor who was always so cool and collected.

As I was thinking of Dr. Petersen, Prodski suddenly moved from the back of my brain, where he lived, to the front, and I thought not so much about unsettling him as doing real damage. Dr. Petersen had asked me the wrong question. It wasn't a matter of hearing voices in my head, of getting instructions from some evil being, as may happen to a violent or schizophrenic patient. It was instead the repeated appearance of this man and the way his image would set me off, shake the stability I'd struggled to regain. The knowledge that Prodski still existed in the outside world, was still dispensing advice, still ruining lives, was more than I could bear. He deserved to be brought down. And it seemed only right that I should be the one to do the job.

Anger was building up in me, filling my being. The blood flowing through me became warm, irritating. There was an almost painful throbbing in my temples, as well as a pounding in my stomach, as if a little demon were trapped inside and striking the walls with his tiny fists.

I knew all too well the signs of being carried away, feared them, feared even a minor lapse. I'd come too far, been through too much to lose myself again. So I sat on my bed—a small but adequate daybed with a good enough mattress—closed my eyes, took deep breaths, and tried to think of something pleasant.

At first I thought of my ex-wife and me strolling down a country lane lined with trees filled with red and gold leaves. The branches arched over the lane, met in the middle, and so created a tunnel that extended far into the distance, like something out of a fairy tale. Only this was not a fantasy. We actually had experienced such a stroll one autumn day years ago.

But the more I imagined Elizabeth, the more she upset this calming picture. For she had, of course, later left me, adding to my misery and causing my already weak mind to weaken even more. So I erased her from this little scene, leaving only me to walk the lane. But then I began to feel abandoned and lonely and what I'd hoped would soothe me now simply brought bitterness and sadness.

Luckily, just as anger was gaining hold again, Carl walked into the room and took me away from the lane and Prodski and the mess of the past.

Carl is a big, round man with rosy cheeks and pretty much looks like what he is, which is German—but the good sort, the kind you can picture in a beer garden laughing it up with friends. He was actually born in Germany, but was so young when he came over here he hardly remembers his native country. He gives the impression of being a lovable fat man, and sometimes he really is. You can see why—when he's not going crazy—he makes such a good salesman, for he comes across as someone you can absolutely trust. But when he gets moody, overtaken by what he calls "the gloom," he can get horribly, even dangerously dark. Once or twice when he hit "the rock-bottom gloom," which he regards as the worst of the worst, he thought of taking his life. Using his knowledge as an appliance expert, he considered committing suicide by electrocuting himself or sticking his head in a gas oven. It's a shame that he can have such thoughts, particularly since he seems built to be strong and chatty and cheerful.

"I'm having a bad day," he said as he sank down on his bed. "I had a feeling it was going to be like this the minute I woke up. You know that feeling? Like you turned stale and moldy overnight. You haven't even gotten out of bed yet and already you're all drained. And look at it outside— it's sunny as hell. Like the day is laughing at you, making fun of you for feeling half dead."

One of the few virtues of being in a place like this, with its assortment of cases, is that you can always find someone who is in worse shape than you are. You can take comfort in that fact, and, if you're so inclined, act like a big brother toward him. For a while at least you can feel well by comparison, even a bit superior.

So I assured Carl that his depression would pass. I pointed out that we all feel somewhat tired and rotten in the morning and dread the day ahead. I didn't completely believe this, for mornings are not the same for everybody. There are many people, settled and happy souls, who can't wait for things to get started. Nevertheless, I thought my remarks rang true enough under the circumstances.

"I was in the dayroom," Carl continued, as if he hadn't been affected in the least by my words of wisdom, "minding my own business, sitting in a corner away from the goddamn sun, and Mortonberg comes over, walking straight and stiff as usual, like he's a general or king. The pompous ass just stands there, with that perfectly trimmed beard of his, which looks painted on—it's too damn black—and he asks me how I'm doing today. I want to tell him that I hate the sun and that he should shave his beard and stop trying to look distinguished, because he really is just a pale, ugly turd with swollen lips and a giraffe neck. But, of course, I have to smile and say that I'm fine and having a bit of a think, planning my day. Like there's so much to do in this fucking amusement park I just don't know where to start."

These remarks and their tone worried me. Carl, as I said, can be a very amiable man and a helpful one as well—he's certainly given me valuable advice on how to please the staff—but when the gloom begins to come over him, he gets frustrated, particularly when he senses that it's going to win out, and he turns nasty and you just know that he's headed for another bad spell. When you come down to it, there seems no easy solution to his problem—either he can sink into sorrow or else try to fight it off by going against his nature and turning into a very angry character. You can tell he's struggling. He doesn't enjoy being mean, but I think he finds it preferable to being sad and miserable and collapsing in tears. I suppose I speak from experience.

I realize that I must be much stronger than Carl at this point because I've given up tears almost completely.

He propped up his pillow against the wall and sprawled out on the mattress, as if he were about to read in bed or listen to a Walkman. But instead he just lay there, still, like a giant overstuffed teddy bear, and stared out at the opposite wall. "Do me a favor," he said glumly, sounding defeated, "close the curtains."

I did as he asked, and they seemed to turn the sunlight blue. I stopped pulling the cord for a moment to look out at the old rooftops across the way. We were on the sixteenth floor and therefore towered above the whole rundown area, which from this height looked abandoned and dead. As did the buildings far in the distance—high-rises, office towers. It was as if we were the only souls left in the city.

I rather like the window itself, or should I say windows, because that's what they are, small square panes of glass, like in an English cottage—only these are set in thick steel frames, which you try not to think of as bars.

For a moment I recalled a quaint little village Elizabeth and I had visited in the Cotswolds—a winding lane with stone houses from another age, window boxes with red and yellow flowers, glass bursting with sunlight. But I couldn't be sure if we had actually been there or if I'd made it all up, using a photo from a book or travel brochure as a reference. Wishful thinking you might say. Yet even London, where I was certain we had been, was hard to get a firm grip on.

Too bad my ex-wife and I ceased all contact long ago. She could have confirmed, or denied, our past.

Carl's state, his silence and stare, continued to trouble me. I thought a distraction might help so I mentioned an ad I saw in the paper for a new, revolutionary, light-as-a-feather minigrill that took up little counter space and came in a variety of beautiful, vibrant colors. Just imagine: a fiery red or sea-blue appliance. Why the thing resembled a toy sports car, or a huge piece of sugar-coated candy.

But despite my descriptions and exaggerated enthusiasm and a subject I thought would be near and dear to his heart, Carl just looked at me blankly, then turned away again and went back to staring straight ahead.

I suppose I got a bit selfish then because I wanted him to be okay just so he could respond to my news. "You've been a good teacher," I told him, raising my voice to rouse him from his mood. "I've followed your advice about how to get on their good side. Yours and Mandy Reed's. And it's paid off. They're giving me a solo tomorrow."

Nothing.

I became irritated. I needed to be acknowledged.

So I moved closer to Carl, until I was standing at the foot of his bed, directly in line of his dumb stare. From having a wall to gaze at, he now had me.

I raised my voice even more: "I've been given a solo pass."

Again, no response.

"Carl," I said, louder still, "they're giving me a solo pass. I'm going out tomorrow."

He stared at me, or at least at my shirt—but it, and I, could have been the wall.

I was almost shouting now. "Look at me," I said. "Look me in the eye. Did you hear me? I've gotten a solo pass. For tomorrow. What do you say to that? Carl? Come on— what do you say?"

As if in a trance, he very, very slowly raised his head, found my face, and stopped there.

"I'm going on a solo tomorrow," I told him still again, but this time in a softer, soothing tone. "They've given me a solo pass."

He stared at me for a few more moments, apparently waiting for my words to be interpreted by his brain.

"Congratulations," he finally said. He then lowered his head again and said nothing else.

Hopeless, I thought. He seemed finished for the day.

That's one of the problems with this place. Cut off as it is from the outside and from all the activities and distractions of the outside, it can cause you to concentrate on yourself, your problems, and your sorry past a little too much. And if you get lost in a mood, as Carl sometimes does, you seem to need more than a doctor or another patient or Bonnie Tyler to pull you out of it.

I left this depressing scene, went over to the pay phone down the hall, and phoned Uncle Arthur. I caught him just as he was about to go off to grocery-shop for the in-valids in his building. Why they can't call the local su-permarket and arrange for deliveries is beyond me, but

Uncle Arthur apparently loves serving as both shopper and delivery boy. I think these jobs make him feel good, mainly about himself, because here he is in his late seventies healthy and spry while his friends and neighbors can hardly walk. In fact, one neighbor, who isn't even seventy yet, is in such bad shape that he can no longer walk his dog, so Uncle Arthur takes care of the dog as well. It's so old that it too can hardly walk, so you might say that Uncle Arthur has his hands full with cripples, both human and nonhuman.

As is usual with my phone calls to him, I hung up so he could call me back and we wouldn't have to deal with interruptions for additional deposits.

I immediately told him about my solo pass and though he seemed very pleased, I got the feeling that he actually found the whole hospital business pathetic and distressing.

Since I wanted to look as fine as possible for my solo and had been admitted to Essex wearing old house clothes, I asked Uncle Arthur if he'd go to my apartment and bring me my very best suit, a charcoal gray pin-striped affair, along with a nice white dress shirt, and my favorite tie, a red knit that had been imported from England and probably weaved, or whatever, in some quaint village workshop in the heart of the country. I remember buying the tie in an exclusive and ridiculously expensive men's store on the East Side as a way of giving myself a treat after my wife had left me. I thought it would pick me up and ward off the gloom—the Carl kind—and make me feel like a distinguished English gentleman instead of a poor, unwanted bum.

"How about shoes?" Uncle Arthur asked, after I'd finished my request list, which also included more fresh underwear. He'd been bringing me fresh underwear every few days. And I began to suspect that he'd bought the briefs and T-shirts in some store since they looked so white and fresh and my reserve at home was so meager and old.

"Shoes?"

"I noticed the ones you have on are all scruffy and cracked. They've seen better days. No offense."

"*Cracked?*" I repeated.

"You know—worn. The leather, or whatever, is coming apart."

"Is it?" With all the things I'd been dealing with lately, I hadn't really noticed my footwear. But Uncle Arthur was right. I was still wearing my old house shoes, which I'd had on since the day I was removed from my apartment. They were dark brown, made of some sort of synthetic substance, possibly rubber, and had developed odd wrinkles, which had become quite deep, so much so that my socks would soon be showing through.

I stood there in the hallway, in the bright artificial light, holding up the legs of my pants to get a better view of my shoes, and studied them carefully.

They were absolutely disgusting. The more I looked at them, the more their cracks reminded me of aging skin, rancid flesh, that of an old man wasting away in a hospital bed, helpless, alone, already long forgotten. I suddenly felt queasy, then a bit sick to my stomach. It got so bad that I thought I'd have to hang up the phone and head for the bathroom. But I concentrated again on our conversation, concentrated on the matter at hand, and mercifully the feeling began to pass.

"Yes, you're right," I told him. "Glad you noticed. Could have been embarrassing."

"Shoes complete the outfit, I always say. You can wear a beautiful suit, but if your shoes aren't polished or are just plain old they can ruin your look. That's the problem with too many elderly folk—they put on anything and end up looking shabby, even older than they really are. I tell them, You have to pay attention to your appearance. You can't just give up. The better you look, the younger and better you'll feel. And people will notice, believe me. You'll be admired."

Uncle Arthur practices what he preaches. The man is always well turned out. Something of a clotheshorse. Though, to be honest, his outfits—the sweater-vests, sport jackets, Windbreakers, and such—are hardly top quality. As a retired postal worker, Uncle Arthur has to watch his budget, particularly since he's so generous with others. Consequently he's forced to buy clothes from bargain shops and chain stores. You might say he looks somewhat cheaply attractive. But attractive just the same. With, of course, a kind heart.

"There's a fairly new pair of shoes at the bottom of my bedroom closet," I told him. "Black leather. They're in a shoebox that says Alden Shoes." I'd bought the shoes for a special night out that Elizabeth and I were supposed to have to celebrate our fifth anniversary. But we never got around to that night. She divorced me instead. "I've hardly worn them, so they don't even need to be polished."

"Sounds good," said Uncle Arthur. "Anything else? Maybe a new razor? The genuine kind this time—a real razor with real blades. Since you're getting all dressed up, you should have a clean shave. If you don't mind my saying, those disposable plastic things you've been using aren't doing much of a job. You always look like you have a five o'clock shadow."

I reminded him that we weren't allowed real razor blades in here. It's disposable razors or nothing. I suppose the doctors figure that you can't do much damage with a small, narrow, nothing blade buried in plastic.

"But I thought that was only for the sick people," he said. "And you're better now. And you want to look nice. Why let you go out if you have to go out with a bad shave? It makes no sense."

Nothing makes sense in here, I wanted to tell him. That's the whole nature of the place. But instead I just gave him the usual routine about having to follow the rules, like them or not.

He then asked if I had a coat or jacket to put on.

I reminded him that I'd come here in my house clothes. And even if the authorities had given me time to select some outerwear, it hadn't been really necessary back then.

I'd been taken away at the tail end of summer when the warm weather was still with us.

"Well, it's gotten very cool out," he said.

"I was out on a group walk about a week ago and it still felt pretty warm."

"Trust me, the weather's changed. There's a real nip in the air now. You can't go out without a coat."

So I asked him to look for the dark-blue raincoat, a London Fog, that I kept in the hall closet. The coat even had a zip-in lining. "I think that'll be enough," I said, remembering that old people like Uncle Arthur tend to be more sensitive to the cold and therefore tend to make a big deal about it. "You can't miss it. It's the only raincoat in the closet. In fact, it's the only one I have. But I keep it clean, and it's fairly dressy, for a raincoat."

"London Fog, huh? Very classy, very European."

"Not really. They make them in this country."

I went on a bit about how disappointed I was when I discovered the MADE IN USA label. As an Anglophile I felt cheated. USA FOG would have been more accurate. Though who'd be thrilled to buy a coat with that name?

My uncle also went on a bit, but about the early bird special he'd had the other day in his favorite Greek diner. He'd gone there with Sam, one of his very few friends who could still walk several blocks. I half listened to what he was saying, because Uncle Arthur loved to talk about the huge meals he got for little money, describing every dish in detail. He seemed particularly excited about the chopped steak smothered in onions that was large enough for two people. "I don't know how they do it," he kept saying. "I mean, how can they make a profit?"

I thought about all the cheap meals I'd been having in neighborhood coffee shops just before my breakdown. After losing my job, I worried about my savings, which weren't vast, and how fast they would dwindle if I didn't economize. I realized that I couldn't return to a job just yet, that there was a sickness in me, in my mind, that had to run its course. This worry would get so bad that it and other concerns would keep me up at all hours, often force me to pace my bedroom in the middle of the night. Is it any wonder that I ended up in Essex?

Having exhausted his food descriptions, Uncle Arthur asked if I needed some money for my solo. I had only sixteen dollars or so in my wallet when I was admitted, and I still had only sixteen dollars or so now. But since I had at least some pride left, I rejected another handout, telling him I'd head for the nearest ATM as soon as I was outside.

"Well, then, I should be there around eleven tomorrow," said Uncle Arthur, "if that's okay? I mean, you'll need time to dress, get yourself together."

"That'll be fine, perfect," I said. "Thanks."

"So do we have everything?"

"I think that's it." But then suddenly a stray thought entered my head and I couldn't stop myself from sharing it with him. I was wise enough, though, to approach the subject in a roundabout way. "Oh, I meant to ask you," I said, though of course I hadn't intended to do so at all, "how did you get on at my building? Have any problems?"

"Why would I have any problems?"

"You didn't see any odd characters or anything?"

"Ran into some tenant who was taking out her dog, one of those little toy things. She seemed pretty peculiar. Looked at me very suspiciously. It was a nasty sort of look. And she kept looking at me, just standing there, until I got into the elevator."

Miss Tice, I thought. A near hermit who lived on the ground floor and always kept her dirty, yellowing blinds tightly shut. The building character.

"No," I said, "I mean, aside from a tenant. Anybody who looked like he didn't belong. A visitor? A stranger?"

Uncle Arthur reminded me that since he was a visitor himself, he couldn't tell a stranger from a tenant. "Why are you asking about this?" he said. From his tone you could tell that he was wondering if I was going a bit off again.

"Well, you can see that there's no security in the building," I explained. "No doorman, no super. Even though there was a mugging in the lobby about a year ago. So I was just wondering if you had any trouble."

"I remember you telling me about that. Awful when something like that happens. Shakes you up. But I've learned to take care of myself."

I was pleased that I'd led him on so skillfully. "So do you still carry a gun?" I then asked, casually, like it was a little, trivial aside.

"What?" he said, quite startled. "What did you say?"

I repeated my question.

"I don't understand why this should interest you," he said, all flustered. "This isn't something I care to talk about. And how did you know about the gun?"

My father told me, I explained. He knew that his brother had taken home some weapons from his war, that one in Korea, and would carry a .32 on occasion. "In fact," I went on, "you gave him a gun once, for protection or whatever. I found it after he died, in a drawer, hidden under his underwear. I still have it."

"Jeez, I forgot all about that. You have to get rid of it. It's unlicensed. It's illegal."

"I keep it well hidden. It'll be good to scare off a mugger."

"Don't even think about such a thing. My God, that's all you need."

"I'm only joking. Just pulling your leg. Who knows if the gun even works after all these years. Besides, it doesn't have bullets. Though I wondered once, after that tenant was mugged, if I could buy some. How would you go about doing that? I mean, you just couldn't go into a store and buy bullets, could you?"

"I don't like this subject," Uncle Arthur said, sounding quite disturbed, even more upset than I'd anticipated. "Let's just drop this now."

To put him at ease, I gave a fake laugh. "It's a joke," I told him again. "Just a little joke. Can't you tell when I'm joking?"

"This isn't something to joke about. I don't understand why you're asking these questions all of a sudden. Are you feeling all right? Is something bothering you? You can tell me."

As I was assuring him that I never felt better, I felt a tug on my shirt sleeve. It was Maria, a little old Russian lady who is always going on about Dr. Mortonberg and how he is trying to ruin her. Now she wanted to use the phone "to report the crook." "He steals everything from me," she told me, as I covered the mouthpiece with my hand to spare Uncle Arthur crazy talk. "Money, stocks, bonds. My underwear is next. He is notorious gangster. And cockroach."

"I have to go," I told my uncle, "someone wants to use the phone."

"Tell your friend this is e-mair-jen-see," said Maria, "that I call police. That there is a gangster here who belongs in prison. A gangster and big son of a bitch."

Uncle Arthur reluctantly said good-bye. The gun remark had certainly shaken him, even though I made light of it again as I ended the call. "See you tomorrow," I said, in a laughing, carefree way. Yes, I was quite the joker, quite the cut-up.

Maria dialed 911, and I moved down the hall toward the dayroom, which was glowing with sunlight and where I heard the TV blaring. Wally was the big TV fan and he liked the volume turned up, despite repeated orders by the staff to keep it low. Although I've come to hate loud sounds of any kind, particularly from TVs and radios, I always seem to enjoy Wally enjoying his stupid programs. For some reason watching this child-man, witnessing his enthusiasm, his participation—the comments, the claps, laughs, moans—cheers me up for a while. I imagine it reminds me of the time when I used to be more animated and involved. At least I like to believe that there was such a time.

I was nearing the dayroom when Tommy Leon called to me. He'd recently become more hyper than usual and as a result had been ordered to remain in his room until further notice, except of course for bathroom breaks. But even at those times he's carefully watched by the staff, as if he's a wild animal that's been somewhat tamed but is still unpredictable. According to Mandy, who seems to know everything about everyone on the ward, Tommy has a history of violent behavior and tried to attack both an aide and a doctor when he was first admitted to Essex months ago. They put him up on the violent ward for a time but when he quieted down and started to busy himself by making weird drawings like a kid in kindergarten, he was considered less risky and sent down to this ward.

So now he stood in his doorway, dressed in his usual baggy commando pants and pea-green army T-shirt, like a soldier from a jungle unit, and called out to anyone passing by who might be crazy or sympathetic enough to want to talk with him.

"Hey, man," he said, beckoning me over, "got a minute? I wanna show you somethin'."

I suppose I feel sorry for him because he's just out of his teens and as such is the youngest patient on the ward, even younger than Mandy, who's around twenty-two. And, according to Mandy, he lives in a dumpy tenement area with no father and a drunken mother and has a brain that's been ruined forever by drugs. Anyway, since I had, as is usual here, time on my hands, and was already feeling more like a visitor than an inmate, what with my solo just a day away, I thought I'd give him a few minutes.

He held up a sheet of paper covered with what looked like graffiti—words, arrows, circles, cylinders in red and blue ink—quite a mess really, an aggressive, violent one at that. "My plan for attacking Iran," he said, and went on to explain that the dozens of circles represented tanks, our tanks, thousands of them, and that they would form a line and sweep down into the country and destroy everything in their path. And they would get air support from thousands of fighter jets—the cylinders—that would be firing on anything the tanks missed.

"Fuckin' great, right?" he said when he finished detailing his battle dream. "We'll wipe out all those fucks. Right?"

"Looks like it," I told him.

"I gotta get this to the army. To the President. They gotta know about this. First fuckin' Iran, then fuckin' Israel."

I haven't been up lately on the world situation and politics, on which country is blowing up which. Obviously, I've had enough of my own problems to worry about. But even I knew that these two targets were sort of contradictory. Then again, maybe such a solution to achieve peace wasn't so crazy—you just kill off everybody who poses a problem until you get peace.

I gave up trying to follow Tommy's similar plans for China and India. Instead I studied his eyes, which were open so wide, so alive with anger. And although they were the eyes of someone who had lost his mind, I admired the passion they reflected. Better passion, I thought, than keeping your feelings all bottled up. As I saw it, this had been one of my problems for much of my life—holding back, allowing certain thoughts and emotions to fester, to expand and crowd my brain until it became swollen and diseased. Perhaps if I'd let out my feelings a little more often, gone a little mad every now and then, I wouldn't have ended up in here.

"We gotta get 'em all," I now heard Tommy say. "Before they get us. Right?"

"Right," I said to keep him happy.

"Anybody else?" he asked. "We gotta kill all the pricks there are. We gotta show 'em we ain't afraid. Did I miss anybody?"

I considered his question, but somehow couldn't think on such a global scale. "We should attack doctors," I finally said, more to myself than to him, "rotten psychiatrists, right here in this city. The place would be a lot better off without them."

He just stared at me for a while, squinting a bit, looking confused. Then suddenly his face beamed, as if he'd just understood the message. "Yeah," he said, "yeah. Doctors! Fuckin' doctors! Like the kind that locked me up. That's a good idea. Why should they get away?"

"There're a few I'd like to see under a tank."

"Yeah. You got a point. Like that fuck who sent me to Courtland. Whoever the fuck he was. Yeah."

"Maybe we should begin at home, is what I'm saying." Admittedly, I was getting carried away. I suppose his craziness was catching.

"Yeah, I hear ya, man. I hear you. Yeah." And with that Tommy slammed his rather big fist into the door frame. "Yeah! Yeah!"

Just then Dr. Banti was passing by and ordered Tommy back inside his room.

"You should not be talking to him," Banti told me as we moved on down the hall. "You should know that by now. We are trying to quiet him."

I quickly apologized.

Banti is a dark-skinned little man with thick eyeglasses. He comes from some underdeveloped country in Asia or wherever, and possibly because of this has even less of a sense of humor than Dr. Mortonberg. I can't afford to get on his wrong side. He'll be one of the doctors who'll vote on my final release.

"He called me over," I went on to explain, though I should have kept my mouth shut. "I was just trying to be friendly." I was almost foolish enough to want to remind him that he and his colleagues had originally encouraged me to interact more with other patients and not keep so much to myself.

"Ignore him," he said. "He is not your concern." Thankfully, Banti left me to stop in at the nurses' station, which is located just before the dayroom. The nurses and doctors gather here, behind glass—as if they're putting themselves on display as normal people.

ON THIS TERRIFICALLY bright afternoon you could get a tan in the dayroom if you so desired. In fact, a couple of weeks back an elderly patient named Isaac took advantage of a string of sunny days by placing his chair by the windows, putting on a pair of ridiculously oversized sunglasses, and basking for hours in the blazing sun. When they finally sent him off to some sort of psychiatric nursing home he looked like he'd just returned from a vacation in Miami Beach.

I took a seat at the long table that fills a good part of the long narrow off-white room. An entire wall is made up of a row of windows, which seem to combine to create one long picture window. If you didn't know better or if your mind was playing tricks, you might think you had stepped onto a sunporch or entered a conservatory.

Although it was hard to escape from the sunlight, someone had pulled a part of a curtain across one of the windows, and I made sure that my chair was in that block of shadow. I don't thoroughly hate the sun, like Carl does when he sinks into the gloom. It's just that I'm not very used it. My apartment, which was the best and least expensive I could find when I was forced into exile, is on the third floor in the rear. It's surrounded by other apartment buildings and as such receives little sunlight. I suppose little is better than none at all, but you can't make too much of a sun that appears on summer afternoons in the gap between two buildings and remains for a mere hour or so before moving on completely.

I must admit, though, that I was never a great one for the sun, never one for the openness of a beach or playing field, perhaps because I wasn't very athletic and looked anemic in bathing trunks or gym shorts. Yes, I preferred the countryside to the seashore. The trees and shrubs would hide me. I could enjoy the cover and darkness of the woods.

Wally Weston was sitting at the head of the table, his chair turned around so he could look directly up at the TV, which is attached to the wall by a kind of swivel contraption. Some big, dopey actor with greasy, curly brown hair and wearing a shiny black leather jacket threw open the door of a big, black sports car and tried to look desperate. Wally had probably noticed me out of the corner of his eye because he turned suddenly and asked if I'd ever watched this show.

"What is it?" I said.

"*Knight Rider.* It used to be on when I was a little kid. They're rerunning it. This channel has all reruns. Some of these things are ten, twenty, thirty years old. It's like being in a time machine, like that one in that movie—I loved that movie, *The Time Machine*. What a great flick. I wasn't sick back when *Knight Rider* was on. Well, maybe a little. I was just beginning. And I wasn't so fat."

He returned to the TV as the dopey actor started to converse with someone in the car, though that person was nowhere to be seen—all you heard was a deep, mechanical-like voice.

"Who's he talking to?" I asked.

"His car," said Wally, his back to me as he gazed up at the screen. "He talks to his car. And his car talks back."

"His car can talk?"

"Yeah," said Wally. "And they call *us* crazy."

I tried to join Wally and lose myself in the program, but it seemed too stupid even to make fun of, and I quickly got bored. On some days I'm able to enter Wally's world, but this wasn't one of them.

Wally is a hard case to figure out. He's a grown man in his thirties, even bigger and wider than Carl, yet he often acts like a kid, so much so that he seems retarded at times. And then just when you think you're dealing with some nine-year-old, he suddenly comes out with a funny, sophisticated remark.

I HAD ESSENTIALLY nothing to do now and didn't particularly feel like dipping into *Oliver Twist,* which Uncle

Arthur had brought me the other day from my home library. So I looked for Mandy Reed, since we seem to have,
for some strange reason, a real rapport and can chat for
hours, but Mandy wasn't around. Which was cause for
concern, because when Mandy keeps to her room it can
be a bad sign. Either she's "flipping out," as she puts it, because of some new medication they're trying, or else she's
just flipping out on her own.

My former wife would be very surprised by my friend-
ship, or association, or whatever you wish to call it, with
a girl like Mandy. She's led a very promiscuous life, beginning when she was about twelve or thirteen. And she
will very freely tell you about that life—going on about
her various lovers: the married men who were twice her
age, the boys who were years younger, the petty criminals,
the drug addicts, a couple of male nurses, a corrupt cop
or two. When she first sat down next to me on the plastic
couch in the dayroom, wearing a robe that always seemed
to be opening to reveal her very well-formed legs, her very
smooth, nicely rounded thighs, she reported to me, a mere
stranger then, how long she'd been without sex and how
she needed it—a lot of it, and with good variety—as soon
as possible. Of course, she didn't put it quite this way, but
instead used a lot of expressions I'd rather not repeat. And
if all this weren't enough, she went on to describe her last
lovemaking session in vivid, almost disgusting detail.

Well, I just sat there frozen, not knowing what to say.
I suppose I was too much in shock to say anything. And,

of course, my brain was still in an agitated state at this time and I was still wondering what I was doing in a place like this, among so many seriously mental people. So I remained where I was, listening to Mandy go on and on. And after a while I didn't mind listening, even though her stories made me blush and took me into a world I'd never even imagined.

Deep down, I think I was glad that someone here, other than a doctor, had noticed me and was taking the trouble to talk to me. Being noticed, or rather not noticed, has plagued me for much of my life. And I think Mandy recognized me as someone who was sane enough to talk to. Because except for me and Carl, there wasn't—and still isn't—any patient you could have a good long chat with. And I got the impression that Mandy didn't much care for Carl and his moods.

We became so chummy—sitting together in the day-room, during group sessions, at the dinner table—that Dr. Petersen took me aside one day to question me about our relationship and to discourage whatever might be developing. Mandy, she said, was a very troubled girl who had been ill since she was very young. I think she mentioned schizophrenia and other ailments. She felt that getting so close to a person like this would be "counter-productive" in the long run. "The girl has a tragic history," she said. "Believe me, you don't want to get caught up in it."

I remember how irritated I became by her comments. Of all the nerve. Who was she to tell me to avoid another person? "I don't understand," I said, "you wanted me to mingle more, be more social, and then when I do you tell me that it's wrong." Which was much the same comment I made to Banti concerning Tommy Leon. These doctors can really confuse your brain, turn it upside down, if you take them too seriously.

"I'm not saying that you shouldn't talk to Mandy," Dr. Petersen explained, a bit annoyed by my protest. "I'm just asking you not to spend all your time with her. I realize that she's very pretty and seductive, but there's also another side to her that you're not seeing." I began to wonder if Dr. Petersen was a little jealous of Mandy, not only because Mandy was so much more attractive but also because she had, you might say, stolen a patient away from her.

I was amused by the thought that I was wanted by two women. I was even tempted to tell Mandy about Dr. Petersen's warning. Knowing Mandy, and Mandy's temper, I pictured her cursing Dr. Petersen to her face, and the two women then going on to have a knock-down, drag-out fight—over me.

You see, I *can* attract other people, I remember telling Elizabeth in my mind. I'm not as lifeless as you claim. I may bore you, your friends and family, and my fellow workers, but there are others—both normal and abnormal—who find me interesting. Take my friend here, a beautiful young woman, with a wonderful face and figure, petite yet solid, with rusty brown hair cutely cropped—imagine, if you can, a very sexual pixie. And she selected me out of everyone on the ward, perhaps even out of everyone in life. And she's a person who usually has sex on her mind, is, frankly, overwhelmed by it. Sex has been on her mind ever since she discovered it, allowed it to rule her, control her, and pretty much ruin her. Yes, this lovely, sex-crazed girl has become my close friend.

Gunshots suddenly rang out. They startled me. For a moment or two I forgot where I was.

The shots, of course, were coming from the TV set. I looked up and saw some man firing a gun at the talking car I'd seen earlier. It was now parked in a dark alley and apparently had just been minding its own business.

"Hey," Wally Weston cried over to me, "you gotta see this. The jerk is trying to kill the car." He began to laugh and then couldn't seem to stop. "Too much," he managed to say between a fit of near-hysterical laughter. "I love it! I love it!"

Mrs. Schulman, a very bony, silent woman in her fifties who looks like she hasn't eaten for weeks, was sitting as usual in one of the chairs by the window and put her hands over her ears to block out both the shots and Wally. I was surprised that she had come to life, even if only to raise her arms. Her husband died unexpectedly several months ago and she hasn't spoken more than a few words since. Mandy told me that they might have to try electroshock if she doesn't respond any better to regular treatment. "I wonder what would happen if you electroshocked a normal person," I remarked. "Maybe you'd turn him crazy."

"Then they ought to electroshock this staff," said Mandy. "Make the creeps feel what we go through."

Another few shots rang out.

"Hey," shouted Wally, who was nearly falling off his chair in amusement, "this guy is really stupid. If he doesn't watch out they're gonna send him to Courtland." With that, Wally broke himself up even more, and Mrs. Schulman pressed down even harder on her ears.

The shots made me think again of the gun at home. I kept it, just as my father had done, hidden away, but up in a closet behind boxes of junk instead of in an underwear drawer. At times, particularly during the period when my mind was coming apart, I would remove the gun from its hiding place, stand before the bedroom mirror, and watch myself as I aimed and pulled the very tight, tough trigger. I'd imagine that the gun was loaded and that I was firing at Prodski in his office or even out on the street. I thought of what I might say to him just before killing him. I kept trying out different messages, the more sarcastic the better, using an expression or two that he himself had used during our therapy sessions, in essence throwing them right back in his plump, foreign face. "I've just become *your* problem," I'd say—a sort of variation on his advice that I had to deal with my peculiar fears and delusions on my own and not expect my wife or anyone else to share them and help erase them. "You should think of this as *your* problem," he'd say, with that little, self-satisfied smile of his, "yours alone, and understand that no one else can make it better but you."

I must have been quite crazy back then, standing there before the mirror armed with an empty gun. Because I had no real intention of going through with the business.

But what if I did make it real? Managed to buy the proper bullets. Managed to work up the courage to take action. I'd succeed in taking Prodski's life. But then I'd have to give up my own. Modern detection and science were against me. They'd put me away for good, for the rest of what was left of my life, probably in a hospital for the criminally insane. The only other option would be to kill myself before I was caught. Which wouldn't be such a bad idea. For my life would then be worthless anyway . . .

I forced my brain to stop these mad thoughts. They were simply leftovers from a once sick mind.

Though I'd lost so much in my life in recent months and had no idea if I could build on all the emptiness, begin a second life, I knew that sacrificing myself for Prodski was not a good alternative.

Yet I wondered why—as I looked about the dayroom at patients who hadn't progressed nearly as well as I had, who were still a long way from earning a solo pass—I wondered why this fantasy remained a possibility in my mind.

WE WERE ALL having lunch when Mandy finally appeared, looking very shaky and still wearing her night-gown and robe, and took her usual seat next to me. There were circles under her half-opened eyes and she seemed in bad shape and, as such, irritable. But I was glad to see her because sitting on my other side was Wally Weston, who had been talking nonstop—saying how he was going to adopt a puppy when he got out, or maybe even a ferret, marry some actress or other who shopped in his local grocery store, sign up for the police and become part of a SWAT team.

Wally likes to eat and it shows. He must be well over three hundred pounds. I reasoned that if he had enough food to keep his mouth busy, I'd have a little peace and quiet for a while, so I gave him parts of my meal, including some overcooked spaghetti saturated with extra-rich, sickening tomato sauce, what passed for a meatball, and a slice of rubbery white bread. He was particularly grateful for Lorna Doones, which came in a little plastic bag and were among his very favorite snacks, even though they were plain and not all that different from other plain cookies.

But unfortunately, Wally continued to talk even while stuffing himself. At one point I tried to get him to direct his nonsense at Mrs. Clarke, who was sitting on his other side.

I rather rudely turned away from him to concentrate on Mandy. I noticed that she had no food tray and was using her table space to rest her elbow while her hand held up her droopy head. "Aren't you going to eat?" I asked her.

"I feel like shit," she said. "I don't know what the fuck they gave me last night, but I could hardly wake up today and felt nauseous when I did. They think I'm some fucking guinea pig, always trying some crappy new drug. I just saw Mortonberg and told him I'm not taking any more of this shit. If he wants to test it then let him give it to his wife. That's probably the way he got her to marry a dick like him."

I suppose I've gotten used to Mandy's language. When she first started talking to me, I was rather surprised that a woman would curse so much, and quite a beautiful woman at that. But just as she was free with her sex talk so she was free with her cursing. If you didn't know Mandy's background, you'd think she was brought up in some poor, tough neighborhood by uneducated, boorish parents. Certainly this was the impression I got upon first meeting her. And when she told me that she lived with her family in a nine-room apartment on Park Avenue, I naturally assumed this was a fantasy. And when she went on to say that her maid was bringing her a few of her favorite dresses later in the week, I was quite sure that she was delusional. Yet the way she talked about the rich and about corporations and corporate executives—she claimed her father was one— made me wonder just how she could make it all sound so personal and real. That's a problem in dealing with people in a place like this—you can't always know if there's some truth in their crazy stories. Well, my curiosity finally got the better of me and one day I worked up the nerve to ask Millie Jackson, the oldest and nicest nurse on the ward, about Mandy's nonsense talk and history. "Oh, it's not nonsense," said Millie, "her sister brought her to the hospital in a limousine." Millie assured me that most everything Mandy had told me about her life and family was true. And Millie said that when Mandy had left Essex her last time around, she'd been dressed to kill, in designer clothes. "When that girl's done up," Millie added, "she could be a movie star."

"You sure you don't want to eat something?" I asked Mandy. "It's a long time till supper."

"I'm getting a fucking headache" was her answer.

I suggested a Coke. "It's good for a headache. At least it always works for me." I offered to go into the kitchen myself and bring her a can.

"I couldn't even keep down straight water. They gave me medication to counteract the other medication. And who knows what the fuck was in *that* crap. This place is colossally fucked up. I can't believe this is the third time I'm in this dump." She turned to face me and managed a vague smile. "But thanks anyway. It's nice to have someone looking out for me. Someone besides my sister, who can be such a goddamn pain in the ass."

"Well," I said, "friends should help each other." I've never been much for sentiment, but I was suddenly feeling sentimental toward Mandy, perhaps because I regarded my solo pass as a sign that I'd soon be getting out of here for good and would then have to leave Mandy behind.

"Yeah," said Mandy, " you're really the only friend I have here."

"It's the same for me." To my surprise that sentimental feeling continued on, even though it seems a little foolish now.

"What about your roommate over there?" Mandy indicated Carl, who was at the far end of the table busy reading the words on his little container of milk as if they conveyed an important message.

"You can't count on Carl. Sometimes he's here, sometimes he isn't. Very unreliable."

"I'd say he isn't here right now. Look at the poor bastard. You'd think he'd never seen a goddamn milk carton before."

"It's hard to be friends with someone who goes in and out so much."

"Well, I've never trusted him. I don't like the way he looks at me. There's something creepy about the guy."

"Maybe he just finds you attractive. There's no one here who really comes close to you in that respect."

"So you find me attractive, huh? You never really said. I didn't think you thought of me in that way."

"It's hard not to notice you."

"Maybe you'd like to do me sometime?" she said, half-teasingly. She even gave my arm an affectionate squeeze. "What do you say? You name it, I'll do it. Whatever makes you comfortable. I aim to please."

I suppose I blushed then and she responded with a laugh. "Hey," she said, "I'm kidding. Not that I'd mind. But you're too shy and too much of a gentleman. That's what I like about you. Even though it bugs me sometimes. Maybe if you got over that ex-wife of yours and that doctor who screwed with your brain, you'd loosen up a little."

I didn't feel like getting into these subjects again. Instead I proudly announced my solo pass.

"Good for you," she said, genuinely pleased. "I knew that you were on your way. I knew it." Then a kind of exhaustion came over her. She crossed her arms on the table and rested her head on them, with her head turned to me. It was an odd way to continue our talk, but you get used to the odd in this place. And this bit of oddness was very minor compared with some of the things that go on in here. I rather like this feature of the place—behavior that might be stared at on the outside is pretty much taken for granted on the ward. There's something to be said for the freedom to act weird, to be among other strange, quirky souls who ignore your own strange little quirks.

"I have you to thank," I told her reclining head. "You taught me how to deal with the doctors. I don't think I would have gotten a solo pass without your advice."

"Yeah," she said wearily, "I oughta write a book. A guide for mental patients. What do you think? Think it would sell? You're a writer."

"An editor, really. At least, I used to be before I was fired." I reminded her of my story, which she seemed, in her exhausted state, to have forgotten for the moment. "But," I added, "I did want to be a writer once."

"So what happened?"

"Didn't have the talent." Of course, there had been more to it than that. Since I'd been alone for so much of my life, the life before Elizabeth, had few friends, and at times none at all, I didn't have much to write about. I'd been too removed from the world at large. My life had been uneventful and my experience with others limited. Oddly enough, it was this very life, or nonlife, that drew Elizabeth to me. "You weren't like other people I knew," she once explained in the early days of our marriage, "I realized that you were different—special in a way."

"I *did* have some talent for art," I told Mandy, not wanting to come across as totally noncreative—as if she'd care one way or the other.

"So what happened to *that?*" She tried lifting her head from the table, succeeded, and then held it up again with her open hand.

"I could copy pictures, but couldn't quite make up pictures from my head or draw things from life. That was all rather beyond me. Although I did have quite a knack for doing faces—you know, caricatures."

"You talk funny sometimes," she said, out of the blue.

The remark threw me and I asked for an explanation.

"All those *quites* and *rathers* that you use. You sometimes talk like an English guy I knew. A real jerk. But girls loved that frigging accent." Mandy then rose shakily from the table. "I'll be over on the couch. My head feels like it's coming apart. And it's too sunny at this fucking table."

Mercifully, Wally Weston had by this time finished stuffing himself and had moved to his favorite chair just below the TV set. There was some old sitcom on that seemed to fascinate him, which didn't take much. I imagine that if you put Wally in a room with a TV, TV dinners, and Lorna Doones for the rest of his life he'd be completely happy and no one would have to bother about him ever again.

LUNCH WAS PRETTY much over now. Some patients had already left the table to return their trays to the kitchen. They then sat about the dayroom or went to their rooms. Others stayed put to sip what remained of their coffee or milk or to stare out at nothing in particular.

I was about to join Mandy on the couch when suddenly the usually silent Mrs. Schulman, who was sitting at the head of the table, let out a long, terrible scream, like something from a horror movie. It caused me to jump up so quickly that my chair tipped over and hit the floor. The woman continued to scream as she pointed to something out the window. Two nurses hurried from the nurses' station to see what in God's name was happening.

There, moving ever so slowly and silently across the sky, looking massive and menacing, was a blimp. On occasion I had seen such craft from the street. They'd looked weird enough from down below and afar. But although this one was probably a few hundred yards away, it seemed close, passing as it was right by our window, and it came across as way beyond weird, appeared, in fact, quite monstrous, a thing from a nightmare. At least that's how I thought of it at first. But since my brain was no longer as fragile as other brains on the ward, it adjusted itself quickly and I was able to take the blimp for what it was: a kind of big, long, harmless silver balloon. Mrs. Schulman, however, continued to carry on and the nurses weren't having much success in calming her down. "It's death," she kept saying, "it's death." For weeks the doctors had hoped that she'd begin speaking again, but I don't think this is what they had in mind. Since she was upsetting some patients, who had gotten up from their chairs and were nervously backing away from the poor woman, the nurses decided to return her to her room.

I looked over at Mandy, who was curled up on the couch and obviously couldn't care less about the screams or the blimp. Considering the kind of life Mandy has led and all the hospitals and halfway houses she's been in, I imagine that she's very used to craziness happening around her, probably even expects it. Wally, though, is a different sort of veteran altogether. He was at the window, almost hugging the glass and thrilled by the show. "Hey," he shouted, half laughing, "it's an alien invasion. Something like in *Earth Vs. the Flying Saucers*. I'm telling you, this is the advance ship. It's reporting back to the others. The aliens are here. They're here to take over." Wally suddenly turned, located me, and asked, as if he needed another kid to play with, "Hey, isn't this too much? Don't you love it? Look at the size of that thing. Aliens, man! Aliens!"

"I don't think aliens would be promoting Goodyear," I told him coolly.

Luckily, the blimp entered a big fat white cloud, and then sailed behind our building and became just a memory.

THE REST OF the afternoon passed quietly. In fact, it was so quiet and dull that I began to hope that the blimp would return or that some patient would, to quote Mandy, flip out and make a scene. But I suppose everyone had been lulled by afternoon medication and was feeling all soft and floaty. Mandy had fallen asleep on the couch and as I waited for her to wake so we might have our usual long chat, I went to my room to get my copy of *Oliver Twist*. I thought I might relax with it there. But the sight of Carl, once again sprawled out on his bed and creepily staring out into space, convinced me to do my reading back in the dayroom.

I sat in a fairly comfortable chair with a wood frame and brown foam-filled cushions, the kind of chair you might find in a cheap motel or hotel, and tried to concentrate on Dickens's story, which I pretty much knew by heart anyway. I'd asked for this particular Dickens precisely because it was familiar and wouldn't put too much of a strain on my brain, which of course had been so overtaxed with other matters.

Once upon a time, before my collapse, I'd been able to lose myself in books and could read for half the day if given the opportunity. My love of reading was another thing that had attracted Elizabeth—still another aspect that made me stand out from the crowd. But as with everything else about me, she tired of this virtue and even began to regard it as a fault. I think the last straw in this regard came when she invited a host of relatives over for dinner—relatives I never felt comfortable with, and vice versa, and who talked to me as little as possible. As dinner ended, everyone remained at the table to chat noisily. Everyone except me. Since no one seemed particularly interested in my presence, I went over to the bookshelf, picked out a book I'd been reading, took it into the bedroom, and lost myself in it. That is until Elizabeth opened the door about a half hour later and told me that this was the rudest, weirdest thing I'd done yet in our weird life together. "But," I said in my defense, "I did excuse myself from the table before I left. I showed proper respect. I did pardon myself." Unfortunately, this remark and its logic only angered her more.

I've tried here in Essex to give myself to books again, fire up my old passion, but somehow I lack the discipline. The ability to focus at length on the printed word has left me. My brain is already too occupied. Far too much is going on inside. So I usually read a page or two and then my attention strays. Stories made up by others no longer seem particularly important. I'm more concerned with my own situation than with the problems of fake people, beings who don't even exist. Their problems can't compete with mine, which are, of course, real. Mine now overpower them every time, reduce them to nonsense. They don't deserve my energy.

But I still would like to more genuinely return to reading, allow it to carry me off the way it used to.

I remember that after Elizabeth ordered me to find somewhere else to live and I went apartment hunting and was having no luck in locating a decent place that was within my means, I stopped in an old bookshop to take a breather and found a book that I'd given up looking for long ago, a story set in the Aran Islands. Such isolated spots seem at times to appeal to me—perhaps because they're inhabited by so few people. And the fewer there are, the less there are to make you uncomfortable. I imagine that those who have accepted such a remote life are quite independent and rather strange and cherish that kind of freedom.

Finding this rare volume, just resting atop a pile of books in a dusty corner, as if placed there just for me, lifted me out of my misery and fatigue. It seemed to magically reduce the loss I had suffered. And for at least part of what remained of that day I felt insanely happy.

MANDY BEGAN TO come out of her stupor in the late afternoon, and I was grateful. I hadn't gotten very far with *Oliver Twist*. My mind kept taking me back to the past, my past, and ahead to the future, and as the time passed I began to grow oddly nervous. It got so bad at one point that I had to get up and walk about the dayroom. I looked out the window at clouds, at a pigeon or two flapping by, stared up briefly at the stupid TV, went through the stack of discs by the CD player, though I had no real interest in them and certainly had no intention of playing any. Afraid that this sort of aimless behavior might be noticed by the staff and held against me, I went into the hall, saw that the phone was free, and decided to appear busy by making a call.

Trouble was, however, that I had no one to call other than my uncle. And I really had nothing more to say to him. So I called myself, hoping that Uncle Arthur wasn't puttering about my apartment. My answering machine answered and there I was, the me before Essex, making an effort to sound pleasant despite a deepening depression and a growing anger. I tried to recall when it was that I'd recorded this please-leave-your-name-and-number message. It was probably soon after I'd moved into the dreary place, alone with my thoughts, noticing every so often footsteps in the apartment above, the muffled voice of someone speaking on a phone in the apartment next door. These people are so close, I remember thinking, and yet their lives have nothing to do with me. Instead of giving me comfort, their sounds added to my loneliness.

Hearing my recorded voice was, as always, a strange experience because I didn't sound the way I imagined. Who was this person? His voice was quite weak and drab, even though he was making an effort here to come across as somewhat lively. I wondered if this voice was also off-putting to others, indicating a man of little consequence, a colorless, expendable soul.

I was so disturbed by the voice and its failure to please that I hung up the phone and called my number again, hoping that I could be less critical the second time around. But although I was now prepared for the voice and its deficiencies, it seemed even less impressive than before. It had no real personality, held no real interest, didn't draw you in.

The greeting was quick and when the beep sounded to leave a message I made up something, just to hear the sound of my present voice and to compare it to the old recorded version. "I'll be home soon," was what I believe I said to the machine, "you can expect me, I'm doing fine." I listened to myself very intently as I spoke. My voice seemed a lot stronger than the one on the tape, deeper, more secure and sure of itself. It had a certain distinction and presence the voice on the machine lacked.

No doubt I had undergone a change in Essex. And with this new and improved me had come a more substantial voice, one with definite character.

But although this seemed reasonable enough, I wondered if I really had changed all that much or simply felt somewhat proud and solid for having survived an illness. And perhaps there was no difference between my current voice and the one on the machine. Perhaps I was simply imagining that difference and once I left Essex for good I'd sound and feel the way I used to and that odd sensation of fading into the background of the world would plague me again.

I was still holding the receiver in my hand when I noticed Dr. Banti emerge from Mrs. Clark's room just across from the phone. Afraid that he had caught me in a weird trance—just standing there, frozen like a fool, doing and saying nothing—I spoke into the phone, pretending to be talking to some editorial colleague, when in fact I was talking to a dial tone. "Yes," I said loud enough for Banti to hear, "that chapter needs a lot of work. Too many run-on sentences. The author needs to break up his thoughts a bit more . . . Oh, yes, that too. Absolutely more clarity, more examples. Absolutely."

I hoped Banti was impressed by my little act, by the involvement that it was meant to demonstrate. Here I was, still a patient, still confined, but already engaged in work-related matters. In a way, I had Mandy to thank for the idea. She'd stressed time and again that the staff appreciated a patient reaching out to the outside world and its normal people.

Well, Banti certainly seemed interested in my conversation because he slowed his pace as he walked down the hall. I knew I could tempt him. Because he's a damn nosy sort, always poking about the ward, always on the lookout for a new candidate for Courtland. I think if he had his way, half the people in the city would be committed to a madhouse. So he must have been disappointed with me—I was now sounding responsible and in command, a model citizen.

It was quite a performance, since I was feeling anything but confident at the moment. I just couldn't relax. My phone call to myself should have served as a distraction, but somehow the doubts it raised caused me even more anxiety.

Was all of this due to anticipation? And was that anticipation positive or negative? Was I simply excited about the prospect of my solo? Or did I fear it?

Determined to get a grip on myself, I returned to the dayroom and sought Mandy's company. Although Mandy likes to probe my past and reveal her own, I usually find our discussions more soothing than disturbing. Perhaps this is what the doctors mean by a cathartic experience. Though I don't think they'd approve of mental patients acting as analysts.

Mandy was still on the couch, but sitting up now, with her legs tucked under her, as she flipped through a fashion magazine. Reading bores her, but she enjoys looking at photos of models and designer clothes. I used to think it unfortunate that she never had much of an education. Hospitals became substitutes for school so early in her life. Although her family had the money to send her to the very best schools, they had to spend it instead on psychiatrists, private nurses, clinics, and medication. And after a while, they became so sick and tired of the routine that they didn't much care where she ended up next and allowed her to be carted off to any public hospital willing to take her in. At least, this was how she described the business to me.

Here she is, I used to think, here she is in Essex when she could be at an exclusive university. But then I began to consider my own education, all that studying and reading, all those tests, all that knowledge stuffed into my brain, and I wondered what good it had really done me. Because here I was in a mental ward, and my best friend was another patient and one whose education had ended in her teens. All those years struggling to add to my intelligence, to advance in the world, and I was now jobless and would eventually return to a dim, gray apartment where I might have to live for the rest of my life.

"What do you think?" Mandy asked as I sat down next to her and she showed me a page of the magazine she was reading. It pictured a long, leggy model in a low-cut black dress so short it could have passed for a swimsuit. "Think I'd look good in that? I'm not tall like her, but I have really good legs. Though I don't have to tell you that. You're always looking at them."

I denied this, of course, but she wasn't convinced. Obviously she had noticed my glancing at her thighs once too often.

"When I get out of here I've got two things on my list. To fuck the first decent-looking man I see and to go shopping at my favorite stores. My mother is trying to keep money away from me, because she thinks I'll waste it on another creepy guy, but what she doesn't know is that I still have a lot tucked away, and the bitch can't touch it . . . Yeah, this dress will have them drooling. One good look and they'll get hard." She sounded sort of dreamy as she said this.

After I went along with her assessment of the dress and its power, we talked about all sorts of things. And the odd nervousness that had been running through my body for half the afternoon seemed to subside. We began to reminisce about my first few days on the ward and our first meeting. And that's when she told me about how she had taken an instant dislike to me, had been turned off by my anger and the way I always sat in some corner brooding and giving other patients creepy looks.

"Was I really that bad?" I said, trying to recall those days, but having a very hard time of it.

"Oh, you were definitely scary. Even I was afraid to go near you. *Me*, who's known every sort of nut there is. And you had those cuts on you, like you'd been in a fight."

"*Cuts?*"

"You remember. The cuts, bruises. One over your eye, another on your cheek." She touched my left cheek with her fingertip. "Here. You can still see it if you look real close."

I ran my finger over the area, but could feel nothing except perhaps a very slight, raised line on the skin.

"And your arms were all black and blue."

I shook my head. A chill ran through me—not only because of her description, which was upsetting enough, but also because I couldn't relate this description to me. Apparently I had forgotten more than just the day of my breakdown. My first few days in Essex had faded as well.

"Come on," said Mandy, "you remember. And your knuckles were all bruised too. Let's face it, you were a mess. But still, you looked sort of smart, educated, and I figured if this guy ever gets his act together maybe I'll have someone to talk to in this dump."

I searched my brain but at first couldn't recall this damaged body she was describing. Perhaps all the drugs the doctors had given me back then had destroyed my memories of that period. And yet when I concentrated extra hard, closing my eyes, squeezing them tightly, forced myself to sink deeper and deeper into that part of the past, I gradually began to make out this man she recalled. He was way back in my head and a bit of a blur, but as I moved closer to him he began to come into focus. The man was standing before a mirror in a green-tiled bathroom, which was very much like the one on the ward, and he was studying himself in that mirror and shaken by the sight. Because the face looking back at him was marked and drained and discolored, an old haggard face on a fairly youthful body. And this face looked very much like mine.

"Where's my head today?" I said to Mandy, in a laughing sort of way. "Of course, I remember. It's just that I haven't been thinking about all of that lately. And when you don't think about something you tend to forget it." I laughed again, rather nervously this time. "Well, that stands to reason, doesn't it? I'm not making sense. Don't know what's wrong with me."

Mandy assured me that nothing was wrong. She believed that my forgetting about my first few days here was a good sign. "When you start forgetting the shit you've been through then you know you're getting better."

"Some doctors believe that you should remember those things. That you have to deal with them to overcome them."

"What the fuck do they know? Why torture yourself? No, Doctor Mandy says that you're on your way. You'll be out of here for good soon. So will I, if they can give me some meds that don't drive me nuts. I'll move in with my sister for a while. She has a place on East End Avenue and can stand me a little more than my mother, who wants no part of me now. Calls me a disgrace, a slut. She especially wasn't thrilled when I picked up some high school kid in the park one day and brought him up to our apartment for a little fun. I thought she was out for the whole afternoon, but the bitch comes home early, sees us all naked and hot on the couch, and goes nuts. Her flipping out causes me to flip out and I start slapping her around. So she finally calls the cops, they take me away and of course I'm completely gone at this point, saying crazy shit, hearing voices, the whole routine. Believe me, I'd live alone if I could, tell both my mother and sister to go screw themselves, but the creeps here don't trust me on my own and won't let me go unless I stay with someone. So it's either my sister's or Courtland. No frigging contest."

You'd think that I'd find Mandy's sordid little stories rather awful and gross and that I'd want to pass judgment—at least in my mind—on the way she has led her life. But I was so used to her stories by now that I just listened to them coolly. Mandy could have been commenting on the weather. That's how much I now took them in stride. In a way, I believe my association with Mandy has loosened me up as a person, made me more worldly, so to speak. Just hearing her stories has been weirdly helpful. Somehow I feel more mature as a result, less restricted, less narrow-minded. She manages to take me away, as books used to do. As I listen to her I travel around the city, to bars and clubs and bedrooms, to hotels and motels, meet the rich and the struggling, the sick and the sleazy, learn about all the things people can get up to with their bodies.

Mandy and I finally got around to talking about my solo, and as I did with Dr. Petersen, I laid out my travel plans. I don't think Mandy found them particularly exciting, I suppose because they didn't include sex, which was what she sought and found on the solo she went on during her last stay in Essex. Apparently she'd headed straight for the apartment of a manic-depressive she'd met on the ward a month or so earlier.

But the fact that the Upper East Side was on my list did pique her interest. She missed her old neighborhood, particularly the shops on Madison Avenue, and asked if I'd stop in one called Claire Dumont's and pick up her favorite shade of lipstick, Parisian Ruby Red. "Only Dumont's carries it and it makes me feel very sexy and guys love to taste it, anywhere I put it." "Sure," I said, though I'd never bought lipstick for a woman before, not even for my ex-wife, and also wondered why Mandy needed such a special fashion item while still on a mental ward. I suspected—and hoped I was wrong—that it had something to do with a young blond cleaning man who'd recently appeared on our floor and had caught Mandy's eye. But I didn't pursue the matter. If I was wrong, I might just succeed in putting a bug in her head. And she had enough bugs in there already.

"Just be careful tomorrow," was Mandy's advice. "I went a little crazy on my solos and it always got back to them—through my sister, my mother, who the fuck knows. So then I come back to the hospital and they decide I'm not really ready for release and lock me up for a few more goddamn weeks. One time when I was on a solo I got the feeling that they sent some aide to follow me because I kept running into this same guy all along Madison Avenue. Maybe it was all in my head because I was feeling really weird back then and didn't trust anybody. Or maybe the guy was just trying to pick me up. Anyway, you never know."

I assured her that I planned to be on my best behavior. Though I thought the promise was completely unnecessary. And I somewhat resented the association. I was on the verge of telling her that I didn't share her obsessions or history, that my sickness had been only temporary, that I wasn't the risk that she was. I'm glad, however, that I kept these thoughts to myself. Why come across as a snob or hurt one of my only friends in the world?

"And whatever you do," she suddenly added, "don't go near that doctor of yours—the one you used to curse all the time when you first got here. I remember he had a funny name—Pokey, Porky, or something. You were always talking about getting back at him."

"Prodski," I said coldly. "The name is Prodski."

Here I'd been worried about putting a bug in Mandy's head, but instead she manages to put one in mine. Because the thought of visiting Prodski on my solo had never entered my mind. It was possible, of course, that the notion was buried there. But perhaps I knew deep down that such a visit would be reported to the Essex doctors and result in my continued confinement, and possibly a trip to Courtland. Or perhaps I knew deep down that if I faced this man again the whole business might turn fatal.

But it's much more likely that I just hadn't considered Prodski as a destination.

"That would be a completely crazy thing to do," I told Mandy, sounding very sure of myself.

"Well," she said, "we aren't in this dump because we're supersane. I just thought I'd mention it."

I was sorry that she had, because as ridiculous and dangerous as the Prodski idea was, I went on to consider it a few times during dinner.

By late evening, however, it seemed to be pushed aside by thoughts of my actual solo, the one I'd pretty much settled on for the next day. I tried to imagine my travels, the feel of the outside, moving among regular people again. I saw myself boarding a bus, walking the streets, entering a store. I began to wonder if I'd be regarded as a visitor, a tourist, or much worse, recognized as a patient on leave from a mental ward. Though the lack of interest I'd generated throughout much of my life distressed me, I didn't wish to attract attention now as a recovering lunatic. Being admired for my worth was one thing. Being noticed for my strangeness was something else entirely.

I convinced myself that such worries were unfounded. I remembered that when I took the subway to work just after my marriage, I imagined that everyone in the car would be staring at my bright new ring and be amused by my new status. But as it turned out no one gave me a second thought. And if people couldn't recognize a newly-wed when they saw one, and a newlywed with such a shiny gold wedding band, how could they possibly detect a well-dressed, well-behaved mental patient?

It was good that I had Mandy to talk with for most of the night.

She left me only once—to go to her room to get the money I'd need for her special lipstick.

"Before I forget . . . ," she said as she handed me thirty-five dollars.

"Isn't this too much?" I remarked.

"No, that's about it."

"Thirty-five dollars for lipstick? For one lipstick?"

"Yeah. What can I tell you? It's foreign, high fashion, all that crap. Anyway, I can afford it. Don't forget—I'm rich."

Yes, as always Mandy managed to take my mind off my worries.

But the medication she was given started to go against her, making her brain spin and causing her to curse more than usual. She eventually got up and walked about the dayroom, then began circling it again and again, like an obscene wind-up doll. It took two nurses to escort her back to her room, which she shared with Mrs. Schulman.

And, unfortunately, she remained there, leaving me alone with my head and its thoughts.

PART II

ONCE IN BED I hoped that sleep would come soon and that it would be dreamless. I needed to rest for the day ahead. In terms of just pure physical activity it would be the most demanding I'd have in two months. This may sound odd, because all I planned was an afternoon in which I'd do a bit of walking, and stepping on and off some buses. But I remembered how achy my legs and overall body would feel after a group walk, which took me only a few of blocks from the hospital. It was as if my lazing about the ward day in and day out had caused my muscles and bones to lose much of their strength.

I tried very hard to concentrate on sleep, to allow myself to drift into a kind of coma. But the tension I'd been feeling off and on throughout the day was now on again, as if it had a life of its own. Although I kept my eyes closed, and my eyelids were quite heavy and weary, I continued to remain awake or at least half awake for a good part of the night. My heart was of no help. It should have been relaxing, taking advantage of my body being at rest. Instead it was beating rapidly, as if I were running about the ward.

At one point I heard voices in the hallway, probably the night nurses having a chat. At another, Carl coughing in his bed on the far side of the room. At still another, repeated wails outside, sixteen stories below—it made me think of a person in intense pain or one completely overcome by panic, by madness. It was, of course, a siren, probably belonging to an ambulance that was just leaving the hospital and heading into the night. I wondered if the person it was sent to help would know what had hit him. There you are one day, going about your business, pretty much in the pink, when suddenly you change, done in by your body or your brain, and you find yourself in the hospital, and hope they can change you back before it's too late. You curse your body. You pray for it. You can't trust it anymore. You can't trust life. It's changed. You've changed. Whether you get better or not, you've changed for good.

Funny that I should hope for sleep. Because there'd been a time not so long ago when I had actually feared it. Back then I imagined that the fading sensation I'd been having more and more frequently throughout the day, the feeling that my body was on the brink of dissolving, scattering, and disappearing into space, would overtake me completely when I was at rest—especially now that I was divorced, slept alone, lived alone, and therefore had no one to answer to when I'd slip into a spell, no one to interrupt it and help keep me rooted. And as the night progressed, I believed that I would in fact fade to nothing, that what seemed ridiculous and fantastic would actually happen. And in the morning the only evidence that I'd been at home recently would be the wrinkled sheets and blankets and crushed pillowcase on my bed.

So I convinced myself that keeping in motion was the answer, keeping alert and active, even if this meant staying up for much of the night. I realized that I'd be exhausted by morning, and hardly ready for a productive day, but at least I'd still be here, still be intact.

This entire problem seemed to have begun two years or so into my marriage. I even thought for a while that it might in some way be related to the marriage itself. Though this didn't really make sense. Elizabeth was a blessing, not a curse. If anything her companionship made me feel more connected to others and to the world in general. For perhaps the first time in my life I'd been able to think of myself as fairly ordinary and regular.

But still there were times during the later stages of my marriage and job when I'd feel that I was playacting just for the sake of trying to blend in with those around me. I'd wonder if I was going against my true nature and personality, that of a lone, independent soul, the character I'd been since childhood. It was as if I wanted to participate but at the same time yearned for my earlier life because I'd felt more comfortable in that life—unhappy and silent though much of it had been. The business was quite maddening. I didn't know who I was, who I truly wished to be.

That's when I began to regard the people in my life (Elizabeth, co-workers) and the places in my life (our apartment, my office) as foreign and strange, and as such rather frightening. And perhaps because I no longer felt very connected to these people or places I'd find myself fading away. It was the oddest sensation. When it would first come over me I'd almost welcome it, glad that I was being removed from my situation. But as it grew more intense and severe and threatened my very existence, it would become terrifying, as if I were experiencing a slow but certain death.

When I went to see Prodski for help he asked if I'd ever had this fading sensation before my marriage and "career." In concentrating on my past, I had to admit that it wasn't something new at all, but had plagued me off and on since I was a child. Perhaps it had simply gotten worse with age. And perhaps I was noticing it more now because it had subsided during the early days of my job and marriage, but when the novelty and distraction of both began to wear off, the spells began to return, and this time with a vengeance.

It was Elizabeth who suggested that I see Prodski. He'd been recommended by her sister Jennifer. Which surprised me. I mean, that Elizabeth would accept a recommendation from her sister. Because the two had never really gotten along. They'd be on speaking terms for several months or so, attempt to get somewhat close, then argue about something or other and not speak for another several months. Elizabeth was the older sister and didn't approve of her younger sister's personal life, which included a lot of men, both single and married, and late nights at bars and clubs. And Jennifer didn't appreciate Elizabeth's criticism. Jennifer is, after all, the assistant director of a high-class art gallery on the East Side and as such is a very efficient, responsible adult. That she enjoyed a carefree, careless life outside of work was, as far as she was concerned, none of her big sister's business. I think Jennifer would like Mandy, though perhaps find her a little too crude and unsophisticated to embrace as a true friend. In any case, she started seeing Prodski because of the crazy thoughts she'd been having after the breakup of one of her longer affairs, this time with a man who had promised, and then refused, to divorce his wife.

Elizabeth probably took Jennifer's advice about Prodski out of desperation. She of course noticed my increasingly odd behavior—all those spells that would come over me and cause me to stare out at her in puzzlement and sometimes fear. And of course she noticed how on several occasions I'd suddenly grab hold of a table or chair. I was afraid, you see, that I might disappear, turn invisible right there in our home if I didn't attach myself to a very solid object. It was either grabbing hold of something or else running from this place that was having such a weird effect on me, this suddenly strange apartment. "What is wrong with you? What?" she'd ask when she'd get completely frustrated and fed up. And all I could do was apologize and tell her that I'd been lost in thought or having a dizzy spell due to a cold or an inner-ear problem or whatever. I mean to say, how could I explain my feelings when I didn't understand them myself? "I don't seem to belong here," I could have told her, but with no real explanation, "and I'm going all light and airy because I don't. Maybe I wasn't supposed to be here, in this world, in the first place. Perhaps it was all an accident." Since I couldn't explain these feelings and since they'd probably sound rather ungrateful and insulting, I didn't express them. At least not to her. But I did tell Prodski.

Yes, I told Prodski just about everything. There was something about his manner that made me freely confide in him. It could have been that knowing little smile of his when I'd reveal a significant incident or when I'd answer a question to his satisfaction, as if he were proud that he'd gotten me to admit to a failing or fear. And his little accent might have had an effect on me as well. It was rather classy, gave his words a kind of weight. He didn't sound at all ordinary, like some common American. I'm not sure what he was exactly—Czech, Polish, Hungarian—but he did come from somewhere in Eastern Europe, somewhere dark and grim and serious. Perhaps that's why he seemed so much in command—he'd probably had a hard life before settling here to study sick minds. He was about my age, a bit on the chunky side, like he was a little too fond of goulash and vodka, or whatever it was they stuffed themselves with in Eastern Europe, and he gave the impression of being older, and a lot wiser.

His office was not very far from our home. And I appreciated the convenience, and not having to travel in a totally strange neighborhood—because as my problem grew worse, I reasoned that I'd more likely have one of my spells in an unfamiliar area than in one that I knew. Long before I'd become a patient, I'd passed Prodski's clinic by bus to visit a favorite bookshop farther uptown. At the time I didn't realize it was for head cases at all but assumed it was just a regular residence.

It was an old red stone townhouse with a striking turret in the West Nineties. Rising up behind it was an apartment complex with a little playground for tots. I got to know that clinic all too well. You see, I thought Prodski could solve my problem. I had complete confidence in the man. I trusted him with my life. And so I increased my visits from just one or two per week to three.

At times the man seemed able to read my mind. He once caught me, for example, staring out at the playground, and startled me by asking if it brought back some memory. Well, sure enough it was doing just that, causing me to recall spring days in high school when my gym class was taken outside to play softball in the schoolyard. The class would divide itself into two teams, but because I was such a poor athlete I'd always be sent to the sidelines. In a way,

I was glad that neither team wanted me as a player because it saved me from making a fool of myself. But the business also made me feel very inadequate. So much so that I had to lose myself in fantasy. As I'd sit on the concrete ground, my back against the wire fence, I'd pretend that I was someone who had nothing whatever to do with these students, someone who had simply wandered into the schoolyard to pass the time of day.

And I believe that's when it would happen, as I'd watch these strangers at play. They'd suddenly seem far away, as if the distance between me and them had increased, and my body would turn all soft and weak, and I'd start to feel a bit faint and then anxious because I was losing control, losing flesh and bone. I could feel the wind blowing right through me as if my skin had become porous, transparent. I'd stand up, walk about, hoping to shake off the spell and become whole again. Sweat would start running down my face and I'd wipe it off and be grateful that I still had a face to wipe. My heart would be pounding all the while and I'd have the urge to run away, but I wouldn't know where to run to. Everything surrounding me, as far as the eye could see—the buildings, streets, shops—looked foreign, unsafe, hostile.

"But I take it that you didn't faint or run off," Prodski remarked. "And of course you didn't disappear. So how *did* you deal with the situation?"

I explained that I'd grab hold of the wire fence, put my fingers through it, and squeeze until the metal dug into my skin. It was the pain that snapped me out of the spell. One day I squeezed so hard that my fingers started to bleed and I had to ask the gym teacher for permission to leave the yard so I could wash them off in the bathroom. How the hell did you do that? he wondered, and I came up with a story about tripping on a broken slab of concrete. It didn't make a lot of sense, since no one had seen me fall, but Mr. Jonas had always regarded me as highly peculiar anyway so he didn't bother to pursue the matter. Besides, he had to get back to his completely solid students.

Prodski wondered if my recent spells were similar to those I'd experienced in my youth.

Well, yes, they were. But I thought of them as a little less intense, perhaps because I wasn't so alone now. After all, I was married and worked in an office. I certainly wasn't as isolated as I had been. You might say that I was part of things as never before.

So it puzzled me that I should be having the spells again, even though my life had changed and I mixed with people more.

"You sound like you see yourself as an alien creature," Prodski remarked, smiling that sly little smile of his, "an alien creature struggling to deal with a new world. You make *mixing with people* seem exceptional, something you must do rather than something you enjoy."

I had to admit that I still had a hard time mingling. I'd picked up that expression from my mother. She used to say, "The boy doesn't mingle well." She'd report this to neighbors, relatives, teachers, strangers. The woman couldn't understand me and therefore couldn't explain me any other way. I was summed up by my difficulty in mingling.

Little did I realize that being so open with Prodski, who continued to dig and pry, was one of my greatest mistakes, providing him with a history that could be used against me. He kept asking and I simply kept answering.

After he'd questioned me at length about my spells, getting all the gruesome details of incident after incident, he concluded that I was suffering, at least in part, from a kind of panic disorder and prescribed the appropriate medication. He went on to talk about "a conflicted personality," problems with "self-worth," a fear of death and "the void."

It all sounded so promising, like he was getting to the heart of me and the cause of my sickness, and I'd leave his office feeling very hopeful. But when I'd return home or to my office and suffer yet another spell I'd realize that his therapy wasn't particularly lasting and that he still had a long way to go in solving the mystery of me. Yet, fool that I was, I continued to have faith in him. He'd become a peculiar kind of friend.

Since my problem wasn't getting any better and the medication didn't seem to be doing much except adding to the softness and weakness I experienced during a spell, I was puzzled why Prodski began to shift focus from my "attacks," as he called them, to my marriage.

I took offense. To even suggest that my marriage was not much of a success seemed absurd. Why, Elizabeth had changed my life. I regarded that evening we first met as a real turning point. And it was she who had approached me. At a book party for a monumental series on the history of humanity that my firm was launching. Though I was just one of many editors assigned to this hugely boring project, I was required to attend. I did so reluctantly. And for much of the night I stayed in a corner of the publisher's posh apartment, sipped club soda, and kept, as always, to myself. Until this softly attractive, pale young woman, with short rusty hair and large, red-framed eyeglasses, came over to me and began to chat away, rather nervously, as if she were searching for a subject that might interest me. I thought this very considerate.

As it turned out, a girlfriend of hers worked for my firm, worked on my very floor, though I didn't know the woman from Adam, and she had invited her to come along to the party—though she was somewhat shy and not all that comfortable in such situations. Well, of course, neither was I, and I very much appreciated finding someone who shared my feelings.

What Elizabeth didn't know, and what I never told her, was that my problem went quite a bit beyond shyness. Yes, I now remember that just before she'd come up to me, I'd been on the verge of slipping into one of my spells. I was standing by a window, looking down at the traffic on Park

Avenue, following the red and yellow lights of cars as they streamed through the darkness, and I began to feel that I was more outside than in, moving through the glass, slowly drifting away, like a spirit, into the night.

So you might say that Elizabeth, without her even knowing it, had saved me on our very first meeting, broken the spell, and prevented it from taking hold—much the way she would time and again in the immediate future. Because we chatted on and on that night, and we saw each other again, and again after that. And so it all began, our life together.

We had, as I kept telling Prodski, an unbelievable rapport. It was quite amazing. We were two rather enclosed people—me especially—yet we seemed to have little trouble relating to each other.

But instead of concentrating on our happy times together—and there'd been many, as far as I was concerned—Prodski was more interested in learning about the less happy ones. And I eventually had to admit that there did come a time when Elizabeth underwent a change.

She started, in essence, to emerge from her shell—or *our* shell, to be accurate. She strove to be more social, establish friendships, broaden her horizons, as she put it. I suppose it was her new job that encouraged the change. She'd quit the small private library where she'd worked for a couple of years to join a public relations firm specializing in the arts. And over the course of a few months, the Elizabeth I knew so well—a soft-spoken, dignified soul—turned into a ridiculously outgoing character determined to fit in, to prove her ability and make her mark. This transformation was so unexpected and extreme that it left me quite shaken.

Prodski seemed amused by my description. This time his favorite little smile came across as more skeptical than just plain sly and self-satisfied. He wondered if I was wildly exaggerating the entire business. Possibly out of a kind of jealousy. And perhaps also out of a fear that Elizabeth was, in her own way, leaving me behind. But, no, I said, there were still traces of the old Elizabeth when we were alone together. More than just traces, really. With me, and only with me, she was very much the Elizabeth I'd always known. It was when other people entered the picture that trouble would start. They seemed to change our relationship. It wouldn't much matter if it was her family, or friends she'd made at work, or people she'd met through other people. She'd always side with them, become one of them. And I'd be left on my own, remaining my usual self—quiet, restrained, true.

Her sudden ability to chat on and on with virtual strangers amazed me, and rather disturbed me as well. Who is this person? I thought as I watched her mouth moving nonstop. At times I didn't even hear her words. I just watched that mouth, and those lips, which were once nice and thin but now looked big and swollen and almost ugly. And, sure enough, the old feeling would begin to take hold in me, the old weakness, the old sweating and fading, and I'd know that a spell was building. And as it got stronger,

I'd gaze at Elizabeth and the people with her, and wonder what in the world I was doing in their company.

A spell could leave me speechless, as it did one evening when we were having dinner with a childhood friend of Elizabeth's and the woman's husband. I think they were called Betsy and Paul. They were back in town for a brief visit and were determined to see as many Broadway shows as possible. And they talked on and on about this production and that, about such and such an actor, such and such an actress. At one point Betsy even sang part of a song from one of her favorite hit musicals of years ago.

I sat by in shock as Elizabeth traded theater and show business news and reviews with Betsy and Paul. Where she had acquired all this strange knowledge was beyond me. Had it been necessary for her job? Or had her past been a lot more active and varied than I'd been led to believe? Or was she leading another life that she'd succeeded in keeping from me? After all, who knew what the woman did during her workday?

Elizabeth gave me a scolding glance, hoping, I suppose, that I'd get the message and join in the conversation. But I already felt like an observer rather than a participant at this table, as if I were watching a little show put on by strangers. Once or twice Elizabeth attempted to more directly force a response by asking me what I thought, to which I either shrugged or said quite honestly that I didn't have an opinion on the subject. After these unsuccessful tries, she pretty much ignored me, as did Betsy and Paul—I sensed that they'd now come to regard me as unfriendly, and rather a snob. Well, how could they have known what I was going through, that I no longer saw Elizabeth as a relation, that although I was sitting before them I didn't really belong, that I had a very strong urge to flee the restaurant?

It was a situation that could only get worse. Because the more I felt disconnected, the more I acted disconnected, and the more reason they had to ignore me and allow me to fade. Elizabeth and Betsy started to reminisce about their school days, and Paul, who had nothing to do with those days, probably felt left out and so he started to reminisce about his. Soon they were all talking about school "characters"—the oddball teachers and the oddball classmates. As they were comparing oddballs, Paul unexpectedly turned to me and asked if I'd had any really classic ones in my school. "No," I said, in perhaps a somewhat angry, dismissive tone, which certainly seemed uncalled for. But I couldn't explain why I took offense. I mean, how could I bring myself to reveal that the biggest oddball in my school had been me?

I had a hard time defending myself when Elizabeth and I returned to the place that served as our home, *my* home, but nonetheless looked very cold and uninviting now, and she went on and on about my off-putting, antisocial, and just plain arrogant behavior among "perfectly nice people." I just stood there or sat there and submitted to the attack, watching again that mouth as it repeatedly moved and those lips as they seemed to swell from the effort. To calm this near stranger and stop her grotesque mouth, I gave up trying to come up with a good excuse and simply apologized, promising that I'd never act in such a way again.

But, of course, as I've noted, I did much the same thing to her relatives just a week or so later. Only this time I went, unfortunately, even further by actually leaving the table and going to another room. Elizabeth remained angry with me for quite a while after that, refusing to say more than a few words to me each day. And when she did speak it was about some minor matter. "We need more toothpaste," she might say, and then lapse into silence. Or "The electric bill is due next Thursday."

During this punishment phase—because that's the way I thought of it—she'd go out without me, meet up with friends from her office at some cultural event or other, even attend art gallery openings with her on-again, off-again sister.

Eventually, though, Elizabeth became relatively chatty with me. I suppose she didn't have much of a choice. Vacation time was approaching, we'd already made arrangements for our trip, and to remain enemies would obviously put quite a damper on a two-week stay in London.

As it turned out, the trip was rather pleasant, despite an unsettling undercurrent to it all. Because in London Elizabeth behaved, for the most part, like her old, quietly friendly self. The anger she'd been feeling for me in recent weeks seemed to have vanished. Or else she had just left it behind in New York.

For an Anglophile like me, London was something of a dream come true, what with all its leafy squares and Georgian terraces, its embankment and river and classic bridges, its bits of history everywhere you turned. I was so distracted that I suffered only a few of my spells, and virtually none lasted more than a couple of minutes. Perhaps because I felt that I'd left a good part of the old me, the troubled me, back home.

I recall one day, in fact, when I imagined that I was starting completely fresh, that all my burdens had been lifted as if by magic. It was an overcast afternoon and Elizabeth wanted to do some shopping. Since I wasn't in the mood for wandering about shops and department stores, we agreed that I would go off on my own, take in a tourist site or whatever.

All I did, though, was walk about, with no destination in mind. And it was all rather wonderful. As I moved through unfamiliar streets and squares, I felt unformed. But in a good way. The past had disappeared. I could be anyone I wished. Even an Englishman, if I so desired. Later, when I returned to our hotel, I was tempted to tell Elizabeth about my spell-less walk and announce that I was cured, that my sickness was over. But I reconsidered my news. It more or less meant that I had to remain in London to feel normal. Remain in London wandering about, testing the waters, so to speak, like a kid trying to decide what he wanted to be when he grew up.

The more I thought about what I wished to report, the more it seemed illogical, immature, and a bit mad. Also Elizabeth didn't appear at the moment to be much interested in anything I had to say. Despite her shopping spree, she didn't seem especially happy or pleased. Suddenly, for no particular reason that I could see, she had slipped into one of her moods. It was a bad mood, the New York kind. I had the urge to protest, remind her that she was in London and therefore should return to her London mood, which had been so amiable up to this point. I kept silent, however, and hoped that she'd tire of the mood and allow it to pass.

That night when we went to bed and she wished me a reasonably pleasant good night, I was fairly confident that she was returning to her London mood. But sometime in the very early morning I was shocked awake by a scream that gave me such a fright I nearly fell out of bed. The scream had come from Elizabeth, who was now shaking uncontrollably beside me. "What happened?!" I cried. But instead of answering she began to sob. I switched on the night-table lamp, hoping that the light would comfort her and immediately dissolve her dream. "See," I said, "everything's fine. You're here. I'm here." But somehow these words only made her sob more. "Must have been a really awful nightmare," I said. But she refused to discuss it. Instead she got up and went into the bathroom, where she remained for quite a while. When she finally returned to bed, she simply got under the sheets and curled up—a signal to me that we should forget the whole incident.

I, however, could not. I spent what was left of the night thinking about the scream and also reevaluating Elizabeth's manner during our stay. Yes, she'd been amiable and all that, a London Elizabeth rather than a New York one, but still she'd kept somewhat distant from me. There had been a kind of pretense at work, a theatrical friendliness, the sort she might affect for one of her firm's clients. And then I remembered our little chat a few days before in a teashop off Sloane Square. I was going on about something or other, when I noticed that she wasn't listening at all, but rather watching me, studying me as if I were some peculiar specimen, an alien visitor. And she seemed rather troubled by the sight, a bit frightened as well.

These thoughts so upset me that I got out of bed, moved through the dark to the window, and just stood there, staring at the garden square below. I could follow the winding path, illuminated here and there by the park lamps, but mostly I was seeing blackness. I imagined myself down in that park, cautiously making my way, afraid of a possible attack by a stray dog or an early morning mugger. Such fears were totally foolish, of course, since the park gates, which were closed for the night, kept out any trespassers.

I noticed that a light rain was falling, and I now imagined myself both vulnerable and wet. As I remained by the window, as if in a trance, I began to shudder. I felt terribly alone. Alone in a foreign room and foreign city.

I turned and tried to make out Elizabeth, lying in the darkness. But she seemed completely foreign as well. And for the first time during our trip I felt that a major spell was about to overwhelm me, that my sickness was having its way again and hadn't lost its power at all. But I refused to fade here, here in London of all places—which I now considered my favorite city, my adopted home—out of what I can only describe as a kind of respect. I squeezed my forearm with my fingers, twisting the skin, suffering the pain until it eclipsed the spell.

Mercifully, the remaining days in London were screamless for Elizabeth and spell-less for me. I was a little uneasy during the flight home, not sure how I should feel. I was glad that the few spells I'd experienced in London had been relatively brief, delighted that I'd been able to stop them in their course. Having such control gave me confidence that I could eventually cure myself through sheer willpower. Elizabeth, however, was another, less certain matter. I didn't know whether to be optimistic or pessimistic about the days ahead. Because as the hours passed and the plane moved closer and closer to home, her mood seemed to change repeatedly, from the pleasing London mood to the cool New York version. It was as if she couldn't settle on a proper state of mind.

Once we were home, Elizabeth had to return to work while I still had a week left of my vacation. Which meant that I had a lot of free time to review the London trip and Elizabeth's puzzling behavior. I couldn't come to any definite conclusion. When I'd allow myself to suspect that something was very wrong with her, recognize the fact that screaming in the dead of night was hardly usual, on holiday or otherwise, I'd then chide myself for worrying about what had probably been just a bad case of nerves, a bit of travel anxiety.

I visited Prodski twice that week. I was proud that I'd handled my London spells so well and thought that he'd be very pleased by my success and newfound strength. After all, he did think rather highly of himself and his ability to reach patients and I imagined that he'd regard my dramatic progress as further evidence of his skill.

Though he did congratulate me, his enthusiasm wasn't as great or as lasting as I'd expected. In fact, he moved on all too quickly from my spells to ask about Elizabeth and me, about how we'd gotten on during our trip. Although I was disappointed by this shift and considered it somewhat beside the point—the point being to deal with my sickness—I gave him a fairly detailed report of our London activities and relationship. But I played down the business of Elizabeth's changing mood and avoided all mention of the scream. He listened without comment as I talked on, my account growing more and more positive, almost making our holiday sound like a festival of companionship and warm feelings.

For some reason that I couldn't fathom then, he wasn't all that impressed by my cheerful scenario. He even went so far as to question its validity. "Yes," he said, "going away, particularly to another country, can be therapeutic. You seem to leave your troubles behind. I myself experienced something similar once." Prodski seemed to hint, as he had done a few times in the past, that he'd had a failed relationship, possibly a marriage. "It's all very comforting, but unfortunately it's usually temporary, something like a dream state. Once you return home, you return to certain realities, and you realize that the problems you imagined were gone actually never left. It's really a very common thing." As I recall he then leaned back in his Danish modern black leather chair, crossed his somewhat chubby fingers and rested his linked hands on his modest potbelly. He sat there silently, again smiling that self-satisfied smile of his, as he waited for me to respond. But what could I say? I was rather surprised by this cruel bit of wisdom. Since he knew, more than anyone else, how troubled I was, why couldn't he have indulged me for a while, let me enjoy my illusions?

But Prodski or no Prodski, those illusions couldn't have lasted long anyway. Because it took me only a few days back home to realize that Elizabeth had returned almost fully to her New York mood and that she was unlikely to change it or prevent it from growing even worse.

So when I walked into work the next week I wasn't in the best of spirits. Elizabeth's renewed coolness toward me had managed to plunge me into a more intense and nasty New York mood than she had ever displayed. And seeing the piles of manuscripts and galley proofs on my desk—pests awaiting my attention, headache-inducing drudgery—only added to my foul mood. I stood there in the doorway of my office, hesitant to cross the threshold and resume my job.

It was more than just the work itself that troubled me. I felt that I was about to adopt a role I could no longer identify with, or at least shouldn't make the effort to fill again. And that's when I spoke aloud to myself, almost unconsciously, summing up so neatly what had been haunting me for years. "This," I announced to myself, but probably shared with others in hearing range, "this is not what I had in mind at all."

Yet truthful and pointed though this comment was, I couldn't really say what it was that I *did* have in mind. No, not for the life of me.

Perhaps this uncertainty added to the wave of panic I was beginning to sense. A spell was most definitely coming on and I grabbed hold of the door frame to prepare for it. I then considered hurrying from the office rather than trying to combat a spell in such troubling surroundings. But just as in my schoolyard days, no immediate destination seemed safe now. And I was afraid that if I did attempt to reach home I'd faint and vanish before getting very far— possibly just outside, right in front of my office building, dissolving in the pavement.

The spell was about to take hold when I noticed something in my office that caused the feeling to quickly weaken. Anger replaced the fading effect, giving me strength and complete solidity.

I noticed that the potted plants on my windowsill and those hanging on each side of the window were in horrible shape, with parched and burnt leaves, many of which had been drained of all life and were now dangling dead. When I'd brought in the first few plants from a flower market a couple of blocks away, I was surprised to see how homey they made my cold, dull space appear. And when I discovered that my immediate boss, Richard Lorch—a smug, officious nuisance—had an aversion to office plants, considered them bourgeois and decorative clichés, I brought in more. "What's the point?" he had the nerve to ask one day when he caught me hanging up a new addition. Perhaps to annoy you, I answered in my head.

That this little garden, which I'd cared for so conscientiously, had been allowed to deteriorate to such an extent I regarded as the ultimate insult, coming from a staff that had always acted cool or just plain indifferent toward me, and as such had sparked a number of my office spells. Fit to be tied, I finally stepped into my office and picked up the phone to berate the staff secretary, only to learn from a stranger—some girl with a Southern accent—that the secretary had resigned two weeks earlier "for personal reasons."

"She was supposed to water my plants while I was on vacation," I told her replacement. "Didn't she leave instructions for someone else to care for them? Leave a note? Something?"

"I know nothing about it," she said.

"But didn't *you* notice that they were dying?" I said.

She didn't appreciate the implied criticism and went on about how she didn't "mess with other people's property," particularly when she wasn't ordered to.

After slamming down the phone, I just stood at my desk and thought of revenge. I'd spent years at this firm, years engaged in editorial torture. They'd taken advantage of my grammatical abilities, my skill in judging the written word, which I'd developed as a youth who often had only books to keep him company. They'd worn my brain to the bone, so to speak. And this was the thanks I got?! This was my welcome back gift?! An office decorated with death!

Here I'd been criticizing a newcomer, when it was the veterans who really deserved my wrath. Hadn't *anyone*, anyone at all, noticed the state of my plants? I began to regard this sorry affair as all too typical. No one cared about my plants because no one cared about me. Whether I was absent or present, dead or alive, made little difference. No one had missed me, nor had anyone seemed particularly excited by my return. Had I remained away, the firm simply would have hired another person to take over and finish the work I'd left on my desk. In other words, I was, as always, completely expendable.

I suppose all of this plant business caused me to think about my relevance at home. Considering the way Elizabeth had been treating me in recent days, which was simply a continuation of the way she had been treating me for months before our trip, I could only conclude that I was expendable to her as well. They don't want me to be here,

I thought, any of them. This shared desire seemed to give even more support to the notion that I didn't belong in their world, that some sort of cosmic mistake had been made.

Suddenly I had the urge to fight back, to counter their rejection. I saw this as a matter of pride, and also of survival. While I didn't fit into this picture, the alternative didn't quite appeal to me. Because the alternative was not being anywhere at all.

"I'm not going so easily," I said aloud in this office smelling of dead plants.

I then had what I thought was a brilliant idea. As I look at it now, it really was rather extreme, and possibly marked the beginning of the end of my sanity. But it did comfort me back then, and I quickly acted upon it. I left my office and hurried to the market where I'd bought my plants a year or so earlier and picked out half a dozen replacements. I remember that as I returned with them to my office I had a savage smile on my face. And I continued to have that smile as I removed the old plants and installed the new ones. "And there's more where that came from!" I announced quite loudly, as if trying to be overheard by the entire staff.

Throughout the week I made good on my threat by bringing in two or three additional plants each day, until my office resembled a small conservatory. Several plants in plastic pots now hung one after the other on both sides of the window. And still another, of the unsuspended, claypot sort, rested in a neat row on my windowsill. There were plants on my desk, on my two filing cabinets, and on the wall shelves intended for books, binders, framed family or cat photos. Having no real interest in horticulture, I had no idea what any of these things were. To me they were simply generic houseplants—a collection of pleasing, though lowly, leaves and vines, sort of mutts of the plant world.

At first the staff was amused by this obsessive display. After all, nothing very unusual ever happened in our office. I think they also appreciated my spirit of rebellion, though not realizing that I was rebelling against them as much as I was against Lorch. They particularly enjoyed the day when Lorch was in a foul mood, having been told that he was falling behind on the History of Humanity schedule, and he took his frustration out on me and my office. "This is getting ridiculous," he said loud enough for all to hear as he surveyed my plants. "This is a publishing house, for God's sake, not a branch of the Botanical Gardens. We're off schedule, and here you are caring for a bunch of weeds. Just look at this place. It's unacceptable. It's crazy. And this business of suddenly rushing out of the office or clinging to walls and furniture—what's that about? No, I'm sorry. You need to see someone. You need help."

I *am* seeing someone, I wanted to tell the fool. And this firm's miserable health plan isn't reimbursing me. It allows for only one psychiatric visit, one consultation. How can any sick mind be cured in one session?! How can you cure lifelong fading attacks in fifty minutes?!

Though the staff laughed at Lorch's blowup, they eventually sided with him. Because the high that I'd experienced from my plant revolt passed in a matter of days and I got all moody again. I'd always been well behaved in the office, quietly doing my work, minding my own business, briefly greeting others with a quick hello or nod of recognition. In other words, I was a model—if somewhat distant—colleague. A gentleman, more or less. But here I was going out of my way to be rude and nasty—giving my fellow workers the evil eye, mumbling angrily to myself whenever I'd walk to the men's room or copy machine or watercooler, snapping at anyone who entered my office unannounced. And if I did leave my door open, by choice or by accident, I'd quickly slam it shut upon hearing any approaching footsteps.

Two weeks later I was fired.

Lorch invaded my garden bunker to tell me. He repeatedly knocked on my closed door and when I failed to answer, lost as I was in a mad mood, he just stormed in. After going on and on about the firm being a tightly knit family, one dependent upon mutual respect, he announced his decision.

"What it comes down to," he said, in summing up, "is that you're frightening people, they believe you're becoming dangerous. And," he added, indicating the dozens of plants, some of which rested on the floor for lack of any more legitimate plant space, "look at what a colossal mess you've made of this office."

Though I was exceptionally upset and protested the firing and even threatened to throw a plant at Lorch, I suspected deep down that this termination was what I'd wanted all along.

As I walked, plantless, from the building, escorted by a security guard, I did indeed feel liberated, but I also felt very troubled. It was more than just my breaking the news to Elizabeth that worried me. I didn't know where I'd end up next or who would have me or if there was any place at all in which I'd fit in better. My mind has done this to me, I thought, using that very same mind to come to the conclusion. My mind, I reasoned rather illogically, has a mind of its own.

I broke the news about my job to Elizabeth, but spared her the actual reasons for my dismissal. Instead I blamed it all on "a dispute with management," "a clash of personalities," the rottenness of Lorch.

Two weeks or so later Elizabeth left me.

I suppose the loss of my job was the ultimate last straw for her, because there'd been several straws before this one that she'd regarded as near final.

Yes, breaking bad news to me seemed to be contagious during this period. Lorch broke his in person. Elizabeth broke hers by way of the printed word. I'd been out early that morning to file for unemployment benefits and when I returned home she was gone. To work. Or so I assumed until I noticed that her cosmetics and lotions and such were missing from the bathroom and that the bedroom closet had been left open and many of her clothes were no longer inside.

Her note, with the parting words, was resting against a pitcher on the kitchen table. It was actually a sheet of copy paper and the message probably had been printed out on our very own computer.

Would it have killed her to write it in longhand? I later thought. Has she grown so impersonal, so coldhearted?

The note didn't say all that much considering the trauma it would create, but what it did say was clear and firm enough. Elizabeth announced that she wasn't the same person I had married, that she had changed. Which, of course, was no real news to me. She went on to say that she couldn't deal with my behavior any longer. "Your problems can't be my problems," she noted. "I can't be expected to solve them. Or live with them." She also mentioned, almost as an aside, that she believed I was going mad.

The rest of the note relayed what might be called practical information. She was moving in, temporarily, with her sister. Which meant that she planned to return to this apartment just as soon as I found a new place to live. She thought a couple of weeks was sufficient time for me to locate another apartment as well as a new job (even if only a "temp position"). As for the divorce, she planned the "no fault" type, which meant that neither she nor I would be expected to provide for the other. I remember thinking that "no fault" was an odd term in this context, because if no one was at fault then the marriage should remain intact.

In closing, she wished me luck in getting my brain in order and expressed regret that things had turned out this way. "I was so hopeful when we began," she said. "But the life we've been leading for the past several years isn't what I had in mind at all."

Although Elizabeth had been featured in many of my spells, had turned time and again into a foreign being, I was rather devastated by her decision and immediately regretted that I'd ever had weird thoughts about her. I tortured myself with memories of our first meeting and the dates that had followed, our closeness and compatibility. I thought of dinners in our favorite restaurant, an Italian place with Chianti bottles hanging from the ceiling and long candles set at the center of the tables. In essence, I lost myself, absurdly, in the romance of it all. A tear or two might even have come to my eyes. I began to tremble. My heart sank to my stomach and continued to pound there. My head started to spin as a wave of nausea swept through me.

I was forced to sit down and get a grip. But I couldn't seem to think of anything to give me comfort. All I could focus on was the disarray, the destruction. I wondered if I had set some sort of record. For in a matter of only a few weeks I'd managed to lose my job and then my wife. What might be thought of as my two links to normality, to a world—however unsatisfactory and alienating—had been shattered.

"I have to hold on," I remember telling myself repeatedly. It was the most I could come up with in the way of a pep talk. The trouble was that there was very little to hold on to now. I'd have to establish myself elsewhere, even if only tentatively, just enough to feel rooted. Either I had to make this effort or else give in to my fear, stop all resistance, and allow myself to completely, definitively disappear, to vanish forever.

I naturally assumed that Prodski would help me in some way. Certainly I expected him, at the very least, to be sympathetic. When I arrived at his office for these post-Elizabeth, post-job sessions I probably appeared disheveled, looking—even after I'd settled in my new apartment—like an outcast, a derelict soul. But I had little reason to feel differently. I thought about the still distant future and concluded that my unemployment benefits would run out before I'd feel sane enough to secure another job. And although my new apartment was dim and nondescript, I thought of it as being a lot worse, almost akin to a tenement flat, and thus imagined that I was now living in squalor. I suppose I began to act the part—of a bum, that is, of a hopeless loser.

Not only was I not taking proper care of myself, but I also was letting my apartment-in-exile go to hell. Dust was rapidly accumulating on the furniture, lamps, blinds, and, as I sometimes imagined, on me as well. And despite my past feelings and doubts, I couldn't deny that I missed Elizabeth, her company, her presence.

So what did Prodski have to offer in the wake of all this wreckage? More or less: "Well, really, what did you expect?" Yes, the man suggested that I'd been hoping for a way out of my life for years, and that I'd finally achieved my goal. As he saw it, I'd never been content with my life from my earliest days and longed to be released. "To do what," I wondered, "to be what?" "Anything but what you were doing, and anything but what you were at the time." He made me sound like someone who had suffered from a muddled brain since birth, and had adopted dissatisfaction as a way of life.

But he considered this recent break as a chance to make amends, because it was so dramatic, so complete. "Yes," he said, "you've really done it this time. Cleaned the slate, you might say." Now, he believed, I could really, truly start from zero, be whatever I wanted, whomever I wanted.

This sounded plausible enough, but as he spoke I kept wondering if I'd suffer a major attack and fade away before I'd even have a chance to develop into this new soul he envisioned. Because if I were starting from zero then this implied that I'd be about as disconnected and vague as one could get, without roots, without a personality. And rather than moving on toward rebirth, I could just as well accept my nothing state and simply await my complete demise.

Although I was already mourning Elizabeth, I expressed hope that she might have a change of heart. To which Prodski stated quite firmly: "You're grasping at straws." He seemed confident that her decision was final, and probably for the best, "for all concerned." He believed that we'd be happier apart, that our relationship had reached a point of diminishing returns, had become just too tense and difficult to maintain. "You'll survive," he said, with a reassuring smile, "trust me. You'll move on. That's what people tend to do. They find other people. For now, however, I think you should concentrate on yourself. You still have a lot of inner work to do."

Prodski seemed annoyed that I kept talking about Elizabeth—so annoyed that he remarked, quite cruelly I thought, "You apparently have forgotten the way you reacted to your wife, the way she figured into your attacks. I would suggest that you liked the idea of Elizabeth and marriage more than their reality."

Perhaps there was some truth to the statement, but this hardly seemed the time for him to make it, and I resented his insensitivity. Couldn't he see that he was only adding to my despair?

Foolishly, I tried to counter his theory by recalling the good days of the relationship, the early, intimate days. "Not surprising," said the bastard, "not unusual. It was the first blush, the freshness of it all. We've all experienced it." I remember Prodski looking away at this moment, from my face to the trees and playground framed by his office window. And I remember that his usual smile disappeared and something resembling irritation crossed his face, as if a bitter memory had suddenly upset his balance and carried him off to another time. Considering the way he'd been treating me throughout this session, I actually took pleasure in his distress, and regretted when it quickly passed.

Prodski would always shake my hand when I was about to leave. I thought of the gesture as very Old World, very Continental and charming. And with it Prodski also seemed to imply that we'd had a congenial and productive session, that I'd be fine, and everything would turn out all right in the end. But on this day I regarded the gesture as hypocritical and couldn't bring myself to take the hand of a psychiatrist, a healer of minds, who'd forced me to reject all my comforting illusions and caused me to feel more miserable than I already felt. I'd entered his office as a wreck, and was now exiting as an even greater one.

I left him at the open door, his chubby hand extended in vain.

AS I LAY in bed that night before my solo, I kept reviewing the past, as if it were important to confront it and exorcise the worst of it before going out on my own for the day. I think I was, in a way, attempting to do battle with my ghosts, my obsessions. To destroy or at least weaken them. To dismiss wrong turns and failures, erase them, as much as they could be erased, from my memory. I suppose I wanted to leave for my solo feeling as cleansed and cured as possible. But I knew that confronting Prodski in my head was dangerous because such a focus could set me off again. When I'd recall those pathetic sessions, I'd become tense and find myself gripping my pillow in anger, squeezing it as if it were Prodski's head. I feared that I'd lose control there in bed, in the early morning darkness, and possibly turn into a candidate for the violent ward. So I now cut short my Prodski memories, because they would only get worse. Far worse. I refused to complete them, refused to remember the story in full.

All of that damn business is over and done with, I reminded myself, trying to be philosophical instead of mental. You've survived and you still have a long life ahead of you. A life filled with possibilities. Achievement. Satisfaction. Joy.

I knew deep down that I was thinking in clichés, sounding in my head like some radio or TV therapist or preacher. But how can you avoid such romantic nonsense when you're determined to comfort yourself?

I even went so far as to imagine how I would turn my life around shortly after my release. I'd find a new, superior job with a salary that would allow me to leave my grim apartment for a truly comfortable, sunlit place, preferably with a terrace. And a park or river view. I'd meet a new woman and we'd have a fine, spell-less relationship. Or better still—and this was really a juvenile notion—I'd convince Elizabeth that I was an entirely new man, solid and personable, noticed and admired by others, so vivid, in fact, that I was impossible to ignore, and she would finally take me back into her life and world.

My heart, which had been all too active throughout the night, was now beating even more rapidly than before. I was so excited about rebuilding my life that I could hardly wait to get started. Raising my wrist, I checked the time on my luminous watch. Nearly six o'clock. Only a matter of a few hours before the entire ward would be awake and I'd begin my solo and perhaps my final days in Essex as well.

I closed my eyes, suddenly feeling exhausted by my nightlong mental journeys, and fell into a deep sleep.

PART III

W ITH THAT SLEEP, relatively brief though it had been, I imagined I'd at last achieved peace and that it would continue throughout the day ahead. I expected to feel refreshed and at ease, and for a time I did. It was only when I got out of bed and moved about my room that the jitters began. Carl couldn't serve as much of a distraction because he was still asleep, lying on his back, his potbelly covered by a sheet, rising a bit, then sinking a bit, a weird breathing white mound.

My jitters continued in the men's bathroom as I washed up and shaved. Such an attack of nerves was similar to the sort I had in my youth just before returning to school from summer vacation. Back then, however, it was more than just a matter of anticipation. There also was a real sense of reluctance and dread. Now I assumed that I was simply overexcited, more anxious than fearful. I kept telling myself this as I worked my plastic razor and noticed a tremor in my hand.

I finally had to grab hold of the sink and wait for the tremors in both hands to subside. "This is ridiculous," I told my body, "you're absolutely fine. We're on our way today. Don't fool with me now."

When I regained control, I went on with my shaving. I kept going over the same areas, pressing down hard on the razor, trying to get my face as beardless and clean as possible. Which is easier said than done when you're saddled with a disposable razor that resembles a toy. In the end, I had to settle for a merely adequate shave because my skin was already burning from my efforts and what looked like a pinkish rash now colored my cheeks and neck.

Since my stomach was on edge and doing sickening flip-flops, all I could manage for breakfast was a slice of toast, with just a thin coating of jelly, and half a cup of coffee. I chided my stomach, but it seemed quite independent, determined to go astray. I'd already taken my morning medication but it hadn't done much good in settling me down. I suspected that my body had gotten too used to the drug.

As I ate at the dayroom table I couldn't help but notice that Mandy was missing. After all, she usually sat next to me. Another bad day, I assumed, though I hoped that she might have just overslept and would arrive late.

But she didn't. And I was hesitant to check on her in her room. Mandy hates for anyone to see her when she's in a truly rotten state and is unable to talk sensibly. I remember feeling regretful, not only because of her bad turn but also because I wanted to say good-bye before leaving for my solo. This, for some reason, seemed important to me. And I could have used her words of encouragement. She was always ready with those. It's a shame that she couldn't apply them to herself.

Uncle Arthur arrived just before eleven o'clock, as prompt and reliable as ever, carrying all the clothes I'd requested and looking rather weighed down by the pile. "Luckily," he explained, as he put everything on my bed, "a friend from the Center gave me a lift." I thought it only fair that someone was finally doing Arthur a favor since he was always going out of his way to help others.

"Max," he said, was waiting outside in his car, so he couldn't stay to see me all dressed up. Actually, I was rather grateful for that. I'd be feeling self-conscious enough without Uncle Arthur's scrutiny. He then quickly opened the shoe box he had carried in a plastic FOOD CITY bag, which was decorated with a picture of canned goods stacked up to resemble skyscrapers. "I hope these are the ones you wanted."

"Perfect," I said as I stared at the black leather, which had an amazing sheen, like a highly polished car hood. The shoes had never gleamed so fiercely. "God, these look newer than new."

"Oh, I gave them a thorough going over. Shoes can never be too clean as far as I'm concerned. They were nicely polished, but there were a few scuff marks." He looked at his watch. "Can't stay too long, unfortunately. Max and I have a long trip ahead of us."

"Going to some sort of affair?" I'd noticed that Uncle Arthur was wearing a suit and tie under his car coat.

"Max is driving me to the cemetery. Very kind of him, particularly since he's a new friend. I haven't visited Helen in a while. In fact, I haven't been to see her in almost three months. And, of course, I'll pay my respects to your parents while I'm there. I miss them, miss my brother. We all got along so well. All those wonderful times up at the lake." I had no idea what lake he was talking about. "Helen was very fond of your mother, you know." Glad someone was, I thought. "They were just sisters-in-law but acted like sisters. Anyway, I like to be nicely dressed when I visit. It's my little way of paying tribute. You understand."

Actually, I didn't. It wasn't as if corpses would notice his clothes.

"I like it that they're all resting together, all in the same place," said Arthur.

Yes, I thought, they can have some lively chats, with my mother treating them to stories about my inability to mingle.

"You should come along with me someday," said Arthur. "It's very peaceful out there. It seems to soothe the soul."

That's all I need, I thought. To have a fading attack in a cemetery. How convenient.

Just then Carl returned to the room, wearing a blindingly vivid turquoise sport shirt that could have glowed in the dark. He was apparently trying to cheer himself up by dressing so colorfully, but for him to go to such an extreme probably meant that he was feeling suicidal. I introduced him to Uncle Arthur, he mumbled an indifferent hello, sat down at the edge of his bed, and stared out the window at what was shaping up to be another of those sunny days he hated so much.

"Nice shirt," commented Uncle Arthur, forever the clotheshorse. "Very festive."

To which Carl said nothing.

"What's *his* problem?" Arthur asked me as we walked down the hallway to the ward door.

"Being alive," I said.

Tommy Leon was in his doorway as we passed by and called out to us. "Hey, you wanna see my attack plan for Russia? We'll destroy the fucks."

Arthur gave Tommy a quick, fearful glance.

"Just keep walking," I told him under my breath.

At the door, Arthur wished me luck on my trip, which I appreciated. But then he unintentionally upset me by asking if I'd shaved as yet.

"Of course," I said, "isn't it obvious?"

"No offense, but maybe you should give your face another once-over."

"If I go over it any more I'll shave off my damn skin."

Arthur could see that he'd said the wrong thing. "Sorry," he said, "I can get a little picky at times. It's just my way. No offense. I know it's not easy for you in here."

"It's not that bad, to tell you the truth."

"I don't think I could take it. All these people . . . Anyway, you'll be out soon. That's a good thing. Just a matter of picking up the pieces, as they say. I remember when you first got here you were in pretty bad shape. I was afraid that we'd lost you forever. But look at you now—all ready to go—well, almost ready." I was still dressed in my old slacks and shirt.

At least someone will miss me, I thought, if by chance I do disappear. But then again, perhaps I really wasn't all that special to Arthur. Perhaps he regarded me as merely one of the many patients he gave his time to. I tried not to pursue this line of thinking, because if I did I might begin to resent him and his motives, see myself as just part of a peculiar hobby.

Uncle Arthur then removed his wallet from his jacket pocket and handed me a MetroCard and a small stack of bills. I rejected the money at first, but he insisted, pointing out that even if I went to an ATM I wouldn't be able to get small bills—singles and such—for possible use as cab fare. "All together you have more than eighty dollars there," he said. "If you don't feel up to public transportation then treat yourself to some cabs. Or a nice meal. Or whatever you like."

I realized that I'd hurt his feelings if I didn't take the money, so I put it and the MetroCard in my pocket and thanked him for his generosity.

We shook hands and I asked one of the nurses just passing by, Nikki Jason, if she'd unlock the ward door for my uncle.

"Oh, I meant to ask you," said Arthur as he paused in the doorway. "That message you left on your answering machine—I couldn't figure it out—calling yourself and saying you were okay . . ." He laughed nervously. "I mean, it seemed a little odd."

"Just testing my machine," I said, explaining that a person could retrieve messages from his home phone by simply punching in a code on an outside phone.

"I didn't know that," said Arthur. "What will they think of next?" Though he seemed to accept my very short and vague explanation, I had the feeling that he was still puzzled by my behavior, and a bit worried about it as well.

I DECIDED TO change in the men's bathroom. It had good, stark, artificial light and quite a large mirror—both very helpful in determining the success of my solo outfit and overall solo appearance. And I wouldn't have to deal with Carl witnessing my transformation. Since his moods had been so unpredictable lately, who could say how he'd react to my dressing up like an executive—and possibly resembling the way he used to look as a department store manager.

I hoped, in fact, that no one would enter the bathroom while I was dressing. I feared criticism for some reason— accusations of pretension, remarks about my turning into someone I no longer was, about being fool enough to try to deny Essex, to leave it behind me.

As it turned out, I myself was critical of my appearance or at least of my clothes, which didn't look as attractive or as fine as I'd imagined. Perhaps I was being too demanding, but I was very disappointed in their fit. My slacks, for instance, used to fit perfectly. Now they were too big in the waist and baggy in the legs. I had a similar problem with my once nearly form-fitting white shirt, which now was so roomy in the collar that I could stick two fingers between it and my neck. My suit jacket only added to the general problem, looking a couple of sizes too big for me, as if it were meant for a larger man, one with more meat on his bones. My red knit English tie remained, of course, unchanged—a badly needed blessing.

This is what misery and tension can do to you, I thought. I blamed my brain for my skinny, pathetic state. But I saw Elizabeth and especially Prodski as culprits as well. Prodski then started to rise up in my mind, but I beat him down before he could get very far.

I had to be thankful that when I put on my London Fog raincoat it covered and disguised much of the bagginess and made me look rather elegant. The coat itself, thank God, was relatively unbaggy, and if anyone did detect the baggy clothes underneath they might very well regard them as a kind of affectation, a calculated fashion statement.

Not bad at all, I concluded, though somewhat insincerely, as I modeled my complete ensemble before the mirror, turning this way and that to get a fuller, more varied picture of this man about town. At the very least I managed to keep my doubts in check and gain some confidence.

I removed my raincoat, folded it over my arm, and was about to leave the bathroom when I decided to examine my face again.

Uncle Arthur, I had to admit, had been right in calling attention to my shave. The five o'clock shadow was still visible and too noticeable to dismiss, and now, what with my elegant attire serving as contrast, it looked even worse than before. This troubled me so much that I quickly went to my room—Carl, luckily, had left for the dayroom—took a small plastic bottle of talcum powder from my drawer, and returned to the bathroom. Uncle Arthur had brought me the powder to use on my body after showering, but I thought I might try it now as a coating for my face—to somewhat lighten my beard, reduce the dirty shadow. So I removed my baggy jacket, rolled up the sleeves of my baggy shirt, and rubbed the powder into my cheeks and neck, careful not to overdo the treatment.

Satisfied, I got neat and tidy again, and reevaluated my-self in the mirror. My face now looked a bit like that of someone terminally ill, but this seemed better than having it look like the face of a bum.

WHEN I FINALLY entered the dayroom, all the patients, except Mandy, were already at the table having lunch. They looked up and saw this tailored thing before them. Some of them stared at me as if I'd gone seriously crazy by dressing up in such a ridiculous costume. Others seemed envious or jealous, as if I'd suddenly gotten com-pletely well, completely normal, and no longer belonged in Essex. Wally was more impressed than anything else, pointing to me and crying out, "Wow!" I could have been a puppy he'd spotted on a group walk. "Would you look at the movie star," said Mrs. Clark. I didn't know if she was being nice, or sarcastic, or worse yet, really serious. "You look like KGB," said Maria, with disgust. "Nice," was all Carl said, his shirt still far more lively than he was. I couldn't tell if he was coming out of "the gloom," linger-ing around it, or sinking into it.

I sat down at the table, out of habit—with my stomach all in knots I wasn't up to eating. I began to feel very un-easy, in a way I'd never experienced before on the ward. Perhaps I suddenly saw myself through the eyes of my ward-mates—by leaving them, I was, in a way, abandon-ing and betraying them, breaking our bond.

No one really spoke to me, except Wally, who kept asking where I planned to go on my solo and giving me various suggestions—the zoo, a pet shop, a Cineplex, Burger King.

Rather than going through a lot of strange good-byes, I went into the kitchen, with the pretext of finally getting some lunch, and then quietly slipped into the hallway and looked about for Dr. Petersen. She was right nearby, talking with a new young nurse in the nurses' station.

While I waited for her to fill out my solo pass I noticed a dopey little cross-eyed plastic figure standing on the nurses' desk. A plaque below his oversized feet read: YOU DON'T HAVE TO BE CRAZY TO WORK HERE BUT IT HELPS. A couple of nurses milling about the station did a double take when they spotted me, obviously startled by my changed appearance. I wasn't sure, however, if they were impressed or just considered this new me as weirdly comical and off-putting. In any case, I turned away from them and tried to ignore their stares.

Dr. Petersen didn't comment at all on my outfit. She seemed, if anything, indifferent to it. At first I thought her attitude surprising, but then I remembered our little exchange from the day before and assumed that she was probably still angry about that first-name business. She refused, I realized, to see me as anything but a patient. I'd probably always be a patient to her—even if I became the picture of normality.

"So," she said coldly, "how to you feel now?"

Delighted, I was tempted to answer, but didn't think she'd appreciate the humor. "Fine," I answered instead, "I'm ready. Looking forward to it."

"And you've taken your medication?"

"Took the morning pill. Haven't had the afternoon one yet." And then I added, ignoring my own advice, "Wouldn't want to become a drug addict on top of everything else."

This attempt to lighten the mood didn't work. She stared at me, blank-faced for a moment or two, and then reminded me that we'd agreed on six o'clock as my time to be back at the hospital.

"You can count on it," I said.

"Well, then—have a good day." She said this with no emotion whatsoever as she walked away from the station.

I had the feeling that she was glad to be rid of me and wouldn't be all that disappointed if I never returned. I remember smiling just then, pleased again that I had so shaken a psychiatrist—because Dr. Petersen and company, notably Prodski, had certainly shaken me enough.

Nurse Jackson gave me my afternoon pill along with a cup of water. She then walked with me to the ward door.

"Have fun," she said, smiling broadly as she unlocked the door. Unlike Dr. Peterson, she was quite sincere.

"I'll try my best," I said, smiling back.

As the door closed I caught a glimpse of Mandy, sloppily dressed in a loose, wrinkled robe, staggering past Nurse Jackson. I tried to get her attention through the little window in the door, but she didn't see me—and probably wouldn't have responded even if she had since she looked quite drugged up and terribly lost.

I just stood in the corridor, frozen, as if in shock, feeling exposed, vulnerable, like a child who'd been left by the side of a road and now had to make his own way for the rest of his life.

First they lock you in, I thought, then they lock you out. This dramatic reversal seemed like a bad practical joke. Or a perverse bit of psychology.

The craziness of it all finally amused me so much that I was inspired to give myself to it and get a move on.

As I stepped into the elevator I thought, They're really letting me go, they're really confident that I'll return, that I won't do anything stupid.

The movement of the car—that abrupt dip that causes your stomach to drop and briefly detaches your head from your body—suddenly reactivated my nerves and I grabbed hold of the support bar for fear of losing my balance.

The door opened a couple of floors below and a red-headed nurse walked in. I'd seen her before, when I'd been down on the medical floors for tests—lungs, stomach, brain. She turned to look at me, then stared ahead, then turned to look again. I smiled to myself. She just couldn't place me.

A doctor entered on the next floor. And greeted me. But I had no idea who he was. "So how are things in Urology?" he asked. "What?" I said. "Aren't you in Urology?" I shook my head, embarrassed yet also honored by the mistake. There was a long pause as the car continued to descend.

"Pathology?" he guessed again. "Psychiatry," I said as we reached the lobby.

I moved through the crowd of visitors and staff, past the lobby guard at the security checkpoint, pushed open one glass door, then another, and stepped into the street.

EVERYTHING WAS TOO bright.

Cars and store windows shined so much they hurt my eyes. Buildings appeared overexposed, vague. I didn't remember things being this way on group walks. There also was too much air about, and it was even colder than I expected, despite Uncle Arthur's warning. It was as if the seasons had changed since my last time out.

I looked up and down the avenue. It extended endlessly in both directions.

There was all this space and freedom, so many possibilities.

The whole business disturbed me. There were just too many choices.

For a while I waited outside the hospital, trembling slightly. I couldn't seem to move much beyond the entrance.

But the very thought of turning back managed to perk me up, give me courage—because in realizing that I could turn back, I was ready to go on.

So I started walking away from Essex, heading uptown. After just a few blocks, I began to feel slightly nervous again. I noticed that I had passed the point where our group walks usually ended. I looked back at the hospital. It already seemed far away. My afternoon medication hadn't affected my body as yet, and I wasn't optimistic about its potential. For all the good it did me, I could have swallowed a glass of warm milk instead. The doctors had a pill for just about everything. Too bad they didn't have one to control you while you watched your hospital getting smaller.

The hard ground hurt my feet, which had grown too accustomed to the nice soft carpeting on the ward. After the fourth block, my soles were in real pain. Yet I told myself that if I just stopped concentrating on the problem, the pain would eventually pass and I'd experience a normal step again.

I followed my advice and after several more blocks I no longer seemed to be suffering.

The area around the hospital had been quiet, with empty, inactive streets except for the occasional car leaving or entering a garage. Now I was approaching a different area which had more traffic and newer buildings and people moving about as they engaged in business and pleasure.

I joined the flow. And no one noticed. Here I was, a current case, a resident of a mental ward, a recovering nutter, and no one recognized the fact.

I was pleased, of course. I didn't wish to be stigmatized. That I blended in so quickly was very encouraging, very hopeful.

And yet—and yet I had this vague desire, crazy though it was, for at least one or two people to give me a second look, to regard me as someone who stood out a bit from the crowd, a man who'd been through a kind of hell and had survived. I've gone through so much, I thought, I really wouldn't mind a little attention, just a tinge of acknowledgment. It was as if I'd suffered for nothing, for here I was, the anonymous soul I'd always been.

I shook my head, as if hoping to dislodge these ridiculous notions, which made no sense. No sense at all.

The light and the cold became less of a problem as I continued on. Neither seemed as intense as before. In fact, the day, the outside, was beginning to feel almost pleasant. "Balmy," I said, as I unbuttoned the top buttons of my raincoat, "quite balmy." And then I thought of how Dr. Petersen would have reacted to such an expression. "The hell with you," I told her.

Since I was doing rather well up to this point, I decided to push my luck and take a bus crosstown to the East Side.

But when the bus arrived at the bus shelter, it seemed too crowded and stuffy so I waited for the next. But when that one came I didn't care for its somewhat worn, dirty appearance and I waited for another. A third bus followed almost immediately, but I chose not to take it because a huge group of noisy senior citizens, sounding like a collection of sick ducks, boarded the bus, along with some near-dead woman in a wheelchair who had to be placed on the lift, which seemed to take forever to rise up and deposit her within. I didn't think that riding along with such likely and imminent candidates for the grave would be the best way to mark my return to public transportation.

Since I was wasting a lot of rather precious time waiting for the perfect bus, I considered indulging myself and simply taking a cab. After all, I'd been given this gift of cash. But then I thought of my jobless state and my dwindling funds and felt guilty about squandering money, even the six dollars or so that the ride would cost. I might very well grow desperate in the future, financially speaking, and even a few dollars might then seem dear. Except for the review of the past I'd conducted during the night, I hadn't been thinking much in Essex about the ruined life that awaited me on the outside. Well, I was now, and a slight flurry of panic passed through me, as I imagined the situation deteriorating further—going bankrupt, losing my apartment, hitting rock bottom. In this context, fading away, evaporating forever, struck me as almost merciful.

Someone then tapped me on the shoulder, cutting short this terrible line of thinking. "Been waiting long?" He was a little old man bundled up in a very worn gray pepper-and-salt overcoat and holding a badly scratched wooden cane. For a moment I couldn't quite get a sense of what he wanted, but then understood that he was referring to the bus. "About five minutes," I lied. "Just missed the last one." The old man shook his bumpy bald head. "That means we'll be here for half an hour. I know these buses. I know them." Of course, I wasn't about to add to his anxiety by telling him that not one but three buses had already passed and that unless some sort of festival was under way we probably wouldn't see another bus for ages.

Several unoccupied cabs passed by and my resolve was beginning to weaken. The old man was moaning now—his alternative, I assumed, to cursing, which he apparently considered unacceptable. I moved away from him as the moans grew louder and more upsetting. But I continued to reject the cabs. It wasn't, I realized, just a matter of wasting money. I was supposed to be mingling with regular people again, getting used to them and normal activities, seeing how I'd hold up. And riding alone in a cab would be defeating this purpose. It also could be regarded as rather cowardly. No, I thought, I wouldn't be intimidated, I had faith in my strength. And so I held firm, determined to meet the challenge.

A small group of riders began to accumulate at the bus stop, and a few of them became impatient rather quickly. But although the wait for the next bus may have seemed long, it was really less than ten minutes.

The bus that arrived was quite new, and looked about half empty. The passengers, from what I could make out through the windows, varied in age. I therefore couldn't come up with even one lame excuse for not boarding it.

As we headed east through Central Park, we maintained a moderate speed, yet this was fast enough to nearly take my breath away. I actually had to breathe deeply several times until I got used to the pace.

From my window seat I looked out at the stone wall of the transverse flying by. Or at least that's the way it appeared.

But this was enough to make me dizzy and queasy and force me to turn away.

You'd have thought that I hadn't been in a moving vehicle for years. But actually it had been only a few months.

The people on the bus were remarkably well behaved. I seemed to find this surprising. None of them talked to themselves or made any strange faces or had any tics or felt the need to rock back and forth or let out a cry every now and then. They looked contented, tired, bored. They were, I concluded, a very uninteresting, unexciting lot.

I glanced at the passengers sitting across the aisle. They were doing many of the things that the people on my side of the aisle were doing—talking into cell phones, fooling with iPads or whatever, reading this and that, staring into space, nodding off. All were enclosed in their own boring little worlds. I had the urge to shake them. Guess where I've been, I wanted to say. Guess where I'm returning to later.

When we pulled into the next stop, just beyond Fifth Avenue, there was another bus stalled directly in front of us. Suddenly passengers from this obviously disabled vehicle flocked onto our bus. Damn it, I thought. Because all of those senior citizens I had purposely avoided earlier were now fellow passengers and they were making even more noise than before, struggling about, dazed and confused, as if they had just survived the *Titanic*.

At the tail end of the boarding passengers was a wiry, middle-aged man in a Windbreaker who instead of moving

farther into the bus stood by the driver and started deliver-
ing a tirade. "What the hell is going on today with you
people? A bus was just pulling away, the driver sees me,
and keeps going. I run for it and he still keeps going. I have
a heart condition. I could have dropped dead right there in
the street. Does anybody give a damn? No, what the hell
do they care. Then the next bus comes, it's filled with a
bunch of yapping old farts, but I get on it anyway. So what
happens then? The goddamn thing won't start. You call
this bus service? Where the hell's the service?"

"Please move to the rear of the bus, sir," said the driver
firmly, "you're blocking my view of the curb."

Realizing that the driver was about twice his size, the
man grudgingly stepped back several feet but seemed re-
luctant to get too close to the senior citizens, who occupied
many of the seats and continued to yap, in some cases about
him. "I could have walked to my doctor by now," the man
said, talking to himself and his watch, but allowing the entire bus to hear. "Look at the time. All this aggravation. I'm
gonna get sick. My pressure is going through the roof. I can
feel it. I'm gonna end up in a hospital today. See if I don't.
Bus service! What a joke! Two fifty for what?! They got a
helluva lot of nerve! Where the hell's the service?!"

He complained on and on, repeating lines and phrases
and refusing to lower his voice. A lot of passengers became
irritated, not with the bus service but with him. A few even
told him to shut up. But in my mind I cheered the man on.

That's it, I said. Don't hold it in. Let it happen. Go crazy.
Join us.

This was the first time I'd thought of myself as belonging to an *us*.

I got off when we reached Madison Avenue. The door remained open to take on new passengers, and I could hear the disgruntled man still carrying on inside the bus. He just might end up on a mental ward today, I thought as I walked up the avenue. Welcome. The more the merrier.

I passed fashionable clothing shops and boutiques, jewelry stores, fine restaurants and cafés. The people walking the streets were even less exciting than those I'd left behind on the bus. Here on a weekday afternoon, a workday for most people, they appeared to have nothing better to do than just stroll around looking rich and tanned.

Yet despite the wealth and pretension of this neighborhood, it pleased me, relaxed me. I felt oddly secure here, felt that it was so posh and orderly that nothing could ever go wrong. I could never go wrong. In fact, I felt more at home in this area than I did in my own. Which could mean that I was really born to be here but through some error I'd ended up in another part of town and in another life.

Everything here also appeared so very clean—the pavement, the shops, the people. A man in a cocoa raincoat passed by. It was the cleanest cocoa raincoat I had ever seen. Later I saw other raincoats almost as clean. I admired such intense cleanliness, but I did wonder just the same if it was a little too obsessive. Why fear a bit of dirt? Why try so hard for such complete perfection?

From my wallet I removed the little slip of paper on which I'd noted the name and address of Mandy's lipstick shop and the name of her favorite lipstick. The place, I was pleased to see, was just two blocks away.

I looked forward to running the errand, for it would bring at least some focus to my wanderings. So I was surprised when I found myself getting somewhat anxious as I neared the shop. You'd have thought that I was a foreigner who feared making a fool of himself by attempting to communicate with a local.

CLAIRE DUMONT, read the lettering on the window, COSMETICS, PERFUME, TOILETRIES. For a few moments I was hypnotized by these gold letters as they gleamed in the sunlight like pieces of an ancient treasure.

The shop was small but lined with mirrors, which gave the illusion of doubling, tripling its size. The mirrors addled my brain, confused it, so I stared down at the counter and cases instead, even though I had absolutely no interest in them.

When the salesgirl, who was indeed a girl—young, but too heavily made up for her age—asked, with a French accent, if she could help me, I had trouble getting out my words, or at least my voice seemed to crack and quiver as I read from my note—with the result that the girl wasn't sure what I'd said and I had to repeat myself.

"Parisian Ruby Red," I said, this time perhaps too forcefully.

"Oh yes," she said, looking at me a little queerly—after all, who gets so worked up about purchasing lipstick. "It is very popular. Yes, very popular. We may be out of stock, but I will see." As she bent down to search a drawer just below a display case, I noticed that the tremor in my hands, which had plagued me earlier in the day, had returned. This is stupid, I told myself. It was as if I hadn't shopped in years. I hit my stupid hands against my thighs to subdue them, punish them.

"Ah, yes," she announced. "We have it. The last one. Such a popular shade, so lovely." Yeah, I felt like telling her, it's for a nymphomaniac schizophrenic residing in a mental ward. I suppose my feeble performance had angered me and I wanted to take out that anger on someone other than myself—preferably a nonsufferer, an innocent.

I reluctantly handed the girl Mandy's thirty-five dollars. You have to be a bit nuts, I thought, to spend this kind of money on lipstick. But then again Mandy *was* nuts—quite literally. Unfortunately, although Mandy had given me the money to cover the cost of the lipstick, she'd forgotten about the tax and so I had to dip, even more reluctantly, into the Uncle Arthur fund to complete the purchase.

Upon returning to the avenue, with the ridiculously expensive Parisian Ruby Red tucked safely in my coat pocket, I continued uptown. My moodiness didn't really leave me, but it was alleviated somewhat by the sight of a bookshop and my decision to treat myself to a little gift, even though my great reading days were apparently behind me. If nothing else, I thought, I'll have a souvenir of the outside.

You could see from the books displayed in the window that this shop catered to the rich. There were a few biographies about society figures and millionaires, a couple of novels set in posh Continental and Mediterranean locales, and a host of coffee-table volumes devoted to interior design, gardening, and country houses. And lo and behold, standing in a far corner, as if the bookseller had been uncertain about its appeal for his customers, was *Arts and Crafts in the Dark Ages*, a volume in my former firm's History of Humanity series.

Although I hadn't worked on this particular book, I hated it just the same. And when I entered the shop and saw another copy on the front counter, I really believe I would have mutilated it in some way if the shop had been bigger and less intimate and the clerks less visible and observant.

I asked one of these clerks if they stocked paperbacks and he directed me to the floor above, which was reached by a rather precarious, spiral cast-iron staircase that looked like a giant corkscrew.

The upstairs area was a tight little space jam-packed with paperbacks, mostly classic fiction and poetry. Years ago I would have been thrilled by such a collection, but now it failed to move me very much and that fact alone saddened me.

Try though I did to work up some passion by flipping through various titles and admiring some of the striking cover art, I continued to regard the books as rather irrelevant—irrelevant, that is, to my present life and recent history.

I then spotted a copy of *The War of the Worlds*. The book had been a favorite of mine as a kid. I remembered enjoying—if that's the word—all the destruction that it depicted, remembered how I'd imagine my mother being attacked by the aliens and crying out to them, "You don't know how to mingle!"

This is the one, I said, taking the book and moving toward the staircase. But suddenly something dawned on me and caused me to back away. I realized that I was alone up here, with not even a clerk present. I had the place completely to myself.

I then recalled that there was no electronic security check at the front of the shop.

It was hard to believe that the owner could be so trusting, but then again his usual customers probably thought nothing of spending money on books. For them this was pocket change, a mere pittance.

My heart was now beating very rapidly because I knew that I was prepared to act on my wild notion. Feeling somewhat paranoid, I glanced out the plate-glass window that overlooked the street to see if anyone in a building across the way was watching me at the moment. I then surveyed my immediate area to check for any security cameras. As far as I could tell, there were none.

I'm simply being practical, I thought. And wasn't this an admirable quality—quite adult and sane? And couldn't it be seen as another sign of my recovery? Why waste $11.95, plus tax, on a book? Why reduce Uncle Arthur's gift so drastically?

Oh, yes, my reasoning seemed very sound and true at the time. But there was also something else at work here. I was excited about departing for once from the straight and narrow. Throughout my life I had struggled to conform to other people's ideas of acceptable behavior, and that struggle had finally led me to the madhouse. I'd been a good soul who'd been allowed to suffer, while truly rotten, unethical, and dangerous beings like Prodski had prospered and would live happily ever after.

Suddenly footsteps sounded on the staircase. Either a clerk or a customer was climbing the steps. It's now or never, I thought. And with that I quickly slipped *The War of the Worlds* into the inside pocket of my jacket.

As I was leaving the shop, my heart still racing, I had to pass a clerk who was arranging some books on the main display table. Out of the side of my eye I noticed him looking at me and imagined that I was about to be stopped. But all he did was ask if I'd found what I was looking for. "It's okay," I told him, "just browsing." I paused at the open door. I suppose I was feeling somewhat exhilarated for having successfully committed my first crime and I just couldn't resist an inside joke. "By the way," I said to him, "this is a delightful shop."

My whole body was shaking now, from excitement, guilt, and an odd sort of pride, and I walked very rapidly up the street as if I still expected someone to dash from the store crying, "Stop, thief!"

People continued to pass by, and I meant nothing to them, as they meant nothing to me. Who needed to court their approval? Why had such a need ever been so important to me? And this particular group was especially pitiful. Here they were, just leisurely strolling about, gazing in windows, stopping in shops, hurrying off to drinks or a late lunch, while a thief and a madman traveled among them, by their side, almost shoulder to shoulder. And the fools didn't even know it. They believed themselves to be perfectly safe.

In my arrogance I seemed to walk with a heavier, more assured step. I felt rather invincible, and this was such a new and unusual feeling for me that I actually had to pause for a while to appreciate it. I chose a bus stop to pause by, because I would have looked a little odd just standing and doing nothing in the middle of Madison Avenue. As I was enjoying this feeling, I suddenly realized how well in general I'd been doing thus far today, without experiencing even one serious inkling of an attack.

I continued confidently on, and soon came upon a shop specializing in paintings and prints. A small watercolor in the window caught my eye. It showed what looked like a tree-lined street of terraced houses. On studying the picture more closely I noticed a suggestion of a railing and foliage, and realized that the setting was a square. A square in London. Much like the one Elizabeth and I had stayed in during our first and last trip abroad. There were several old prints in the window as well, all apparently of English subjects—a market town, a country church and church-yard, a big crowded train station, possibly Victoria.

England, and the past, seemed to be calling, so I boldly entered the shop, which was filled with similar images. A distinguished gentleman with meticulously combed white hair came over to me as I surveyed the collection. He was tanned and very clean.

"Yes, that one is particularly beautiful," he said, refer-ring to a small painting of a field with cows that I seemed to be facing at the moment. "Top quality there."

"Oh, I'm sure," I said, just to say something.

"Comparable to early Constable, as far as I'm concerned."

"Yes, you may be right, " I said, though I hardly knew anything about Constable, much less early Constable.

"No question about it. Sir Edmund Howard. Got rather lost in the shuffle, which is regrettable, but you can see the skill, the touch."

"Most definitely."

"And for only nine thousand it's a unique bargain, abso-lutely unique."

"Seems so," I said, trying to sound as noncommittal as possible while still coming across as a serious collector.

The man obviously recognized my hesitancy, but re-fused to be discouraged. "I have some interesting things in the back," he said. "Let me show them to you."

I could have gracefully excused myself, citing a tight schedule or some such nonsense, but I was rather enjoying this little game of dress-up and pretend, and wanted to play more. At the same time, I was quite amazed and disgusted by the entire business—that there actually were people who led the kind of life that allowed them to look at pictures all afternoon, and that there actually were merchants to indulge them in this folly. It all seemed so terribly extravagant and unfair. Unfair, I mean to say, to those of us who have to struggle just to get through a day.

He guided me to an office that had many framed pictures resting against the walls, and held up several for my approval. When I seemed somewhat lukewarm about those, he held up several more. I stopped at one, a drawing of what looked like the famous crescent in Bath. Elizabeth and I had put Bath on our itinerary, but had never gotten around to it. It was a very realistic, very detailed image, and I gazed at it steadily, and could imagine myself in the picture, right there in Bath, touring the city, strolling along the crescent.

"Ah, yes," said the man, "very appealing, isn't it? I can see the light in your eyes. Lovely when that happens. And I believe—let's see here—yes, I was right—it's only eleven thousand. Beautifully done. Early nineteenth century. Real charm there. In wonderful condition. You couldn't do better."

I wanted to say how nice the picture would look in my room back on the mental ward and wanted to ask if he might lower the price to, say, fifteen dollars. But I told him instead that I'd have to think about it.

He handed me his card. "Don't wait too long," he warned. "This may not be here tomorrow."

I may not be here tomorrow, I wanted to tell him.

SINCE I'D ADAPTED so well to passing time like the idle rich, I decided to visit some of the full-scale art galleries in the area. I've always appreciated literature, but could never get all that enthusiastic about pictures on a wall, particularly the modern sort with scribbles, squiggles, and blobs that looked like diseased thoughts. But now I figured, When in Rome, etc.

I must have looked fairly distinguished because the gallery people greeted me pleasantly, with respect. My London Fog and my baggy ensemble underneath were going over quite well. Although I didn't own many clothes, I apparently had exceptional taste.

In one of the galleries there were huge canvases with paint splattered all about and ugly heads and twisted bodies caught up in each individual mess. I think the artist was trying to come off as disturbed. He should have seen the group mural we did one day in occupational therapy. Each patient, one at a time, went up to a big and very long sheet of paper taped to the wall and drew whatever his sick mind told him. There was Wally's sloppy puppy, Mrs. Clark's amoeba designs, Carl's frying pan, Mrs. Schulman's happy man with mustache and glasses, Mandy's nude boy with giant penis, Tommy Leon's explosions, Maria's Russian fur hat, and my Big Ben. Seeing all of this strangeness crowded together made you feel a bit nauseous. But at least it was genuine, not some arty pose. It was what *disturbed* was all about.

I not only explored Madison Avenue, but also turned into the side streets, where there were galleries in fabulous, beautifully kept townhouses—meticulous residences for meticulous people. One particularly exclusive gallery even employed a guard, who held open the door for me and wished me a good day.

When I routinely rounded still another corner to visit still another gallery, my stomach suddenly sank. And my heart skipped several beats. And I began to feel vaguely ill. For by pure chance, I found myself on a familiar block and just one house away from an all-too-familiar street-level gallery.

THIS WAS WHERE Jennifer, Elizabeth's sister, worked and where I'd met her many months before to discuss the collapse of my marriage, my exile, and the current state of Elizabeth's brain. I'd never been close to Jennifer—in fact, I rarely saw her. But when Elizabeth stopped speaking to me entirely, rejecting all attempts at contact, I became more desperate than ever. You see, I had the absurd idea that even though Elizabeth had divorced me, we could still, as they say, "patch things up." Obviously, if she was unwilling to talk with me, we couldn't begin "the healing process." I therefore reasoned, not very logically, that her closest relation would be the next-best person to approach.

I suppose that I sorely needed some guidance. Certainly Prodski had been of little help. And by this time he wasn't even an option since I'd given up seeing him because of the expense.

Luckily, Elizabeth and Jennifer had just had one of their periodic fights, so when I phoned Jennifer she could identify with my distress. Although she'd always regarded me as rather a mysterious, shadowy character, she probably felt that we were now comrades, since both of us had been wronged by her sister. In any case, she suggested we meet for lunch and asked me to wait for her outside her gallery.

We walked a few blocks to a French café, which looked weirdly out of place, as if had been extracted from Paris and plopped down here. For what it was—a cramped space with average food—the café was quite overpriced. But Jennifer told me not to worry since she planned to charge the lunch as a business expense.

I recall how unsettling it was to sit across from her. Because she seemed like a more fashionable, worldly, and somewhat broader version of Elizabeth—someone playing Elizabeth as a sophisticate. She was certainly more animated than her sister, often brushing back one of her dyed blond curls from her face, and taking a drag from a cigarette almost every time she completed several sentences.

Elizabeth had often criticized Jennifer for her smoking and drinking habits, and this had caused a number of rather heated arguments.

After telling me, rather bluntly, that I wasn't looking so good, she went on to rail against Elizabeth's demanding character and to say how sorry she was that she and I had to suffer because of that character.

"We all have our faults or little weaknesses," she remarked, "but Liz magnifies them and becomes impossibly intolerant. I mean, look at what she did to you. You have, from what I understand, a nervous sort of thing going on. No big deal, right? We're all nervous wrecks in this city— some worse than others, of course." She probably puffed on her cigarette then. "God, but I'm sorry that I ever mentioned Prodski to her. He can be such a pompous ass at times, but I really thought he might help you. Who knew that he'd start meddling in your marriage."

I was about to raise another piece of cheese omelet to my mouth, but this remark caused me to lower my fork. "I'm not following," I said. "What do you mean by *meddling*?"

"Oh, you know, all that advice Prodski gave Liz. Of course, he refuses to see it as advice. He likes to believe that he just inspires you to make the right decision, to think for yourself. Doesn't want to come across as controlling. Wants to remain objective. But considering how he dealt with you and Liz, you can see what a lot of crap that is."

At first I was sure that she had her facts wrong, that she was under the mistaken impression that Elizabeth and I had gone to Prodski together. "But I went to Prodski alone," I told her. "Always alone. Elizabeth never went with me."

"You mean she never told you?" Jennifer sounded quite startled. "Even after she left you? I know she kept it from you while you were still together or at least still speaking. I suppose that was understandable, in a way. But even after everything was over—nothing? Not a word?"

"Kept *what* from me? What are you talking about?"

That's when she told me the whole rotten story. It seems that shortly after I'd begun seeing Prodski about my attacks, Elizabeth had gone to him, as a kind of patient, to discuss her frustration with me, the prognosis for my future, and whether or not she should leave me. She seemed to fear a loss of her own sanity if she continued on as usual.

"Liz didn't even tell me about these sessions until everything was pretty much over. Didn't tell *me*, you understand— *me* who'd recommended Prodski in the first place. How secretive can you get? I ask you."

I couldn't speak. I suppose I turned pale and looked faint because Jennifer repeatedly asked if I was okay. The omelet felt as if it had curdled in my stomach and I thought I might vomit at any moment. The sense of betrayal— the thought that all those discussions had gone on behind my back, discussions on how best to be rid of me—was overwhelming. Elizabeth's actions were bad enough, but Prodski's behavior, the sheer hypocrisy of it all, the blatant violation of ethics, was appalling, cause for prosecution or, better still, execution.

I had to make a real effort to remain at the table, to continue to act civilly and sanely. Because all the hurt that ran through me was soon replaced by rage and I had the urge to immediately go to Prodski's office and explode.

Jennifer's further remarks only incited me more. "And of course," she said, as if thinking aloud, "when you tell him about a troubled relationship his solution is basically to end it. His philosophy is why make an effort when the thing is already so damaged. That's very much what he put in my head when I was involved with Martin. And you have to give him credit—he does practice what he preaches. I mean, I gathered from him, in so many words, that he divorced his wife because their relationship had become too difficult. Of course, I later found out, from someone who knows Prodski, that he left her for a supposedly cute colleague who's something like fifteen years younger."

"Why then," I asked, not very successfully containing my anger, this time directed toward her, "why, knowing all of this, did you recommend him to Elizabeth?"

"I heard that he was good with nervous disorders as well as relationships. And since he helped me get over my relationship, I thought he'd be just as helpful when it came to nervous problems. But I recommended him for you, not for Elizabeth—for a nervous condition, not a relationship problem. Who knew that Elizabeth would go to see him on her own? Go to see him about you."

I began to recall some of Elizabeth's words when she'd talked about our problems, about my attitude and my spells. I now understood why they'd sounded so familiar at the time. The phrases, expressions, reasoning had come from Prodski. She'd been programmed, brainwashed by the bastard. Yes, of course. It was so obvious now. In her parting letter she'd said that my problems couldn't be her problems. No wonder I'd felt that I'd come across a similar line before. It was a classic Prodski-ism. And no wonder Prodski tried to convince me that divorce wasn't such a bad thing. He was secretly acting on Elizabeth's behalf. Although he pretended to have my best interests at heart, he had secretly switched alliances, and now saw me as hopeless and expendable. Perhaps he hoped that I would indeed disappear.

I fumed as I sat in that imitation bistro. "All of you want me to go," I said to Jennifer, between my teeth. I then held up my hand in front of her. "Feel it," I ordered, "it's solid. And so is the rest of me. Skin, bones. I'm here. And I'm not going to disappear just to please you. Feel it!"

Jennifer backed her chair away from the table, preparing to escape if necessary. But she glanced about her, at the other patrons, and you could see that she didn't want us to create a scene and so she gave a fake smile and nod and asked me under her breath to please quiet down and control myself.

I did lower my voice, but I couldn't stop my thoughts, which were jumbled, all senseless bits and pieces. "What am I doing here, in this place? What am I doing here with you? You—who sent me to Prodski. But it's not only you. It's all of you. I'm a bother, a nuisance. I make you uncomfortable. I don't fit into your scheme. So I'll make you happy now. I'll leave you behind, all of you. But I'm not leaving this world. I won't give you that satisfaction. I don't know why I'm here, but now that I am, I'm staying. And people will regret what they've done. They're going to pay for their actions. Mark my words."

I'm sure that Jennifer switched sides at this moment. She hardly needed any more convincing that her sister had done the right thing. Poor Liz had been living with a bloody lunatic!

"I'll skip desert and coffee, if you don't mind," I growled at her and hurried from the café.

I moved about in an angry daze, wanting to strike out at someone, something, anything, but I was unable to focus. I began to curse, which was so unlike me, curse aloud as I walked toward Fifth Avenue and the lush green of Central Park. There were only a few pedestrians along the entire length of the street. But this block between Madison and Fifth, with one luxurious townhouse following another, was generally quiet and still, which was the way the rich apparently liked it. I suppose it was lucky that I was doing my cursing and ranting here, because if I'd been on the far more populated Madison Avenue the police might very well have been called. The rich do not tolerate crazies on their streets. I did, however, manage to startle a couple who passed by. They expressed their disapproval in what sounded like French. Otherwise I was only heard by birds chirping in the trees that lined the dead block.

He's destroyed my normal life, I kept thinking—that part of my life that made me appear average, regular, wanted. He subverted it, infected it until it was no more. I imagined him telling Elizabeth that my problem was irreversible, that my spells were a kind of madness that had been with me since youth, that I'd become conditioned to them, that they'd become a part of me, and that she had to escape to preserve her own mental health.

As I neared Fifth Avenue, I finally questioned where I was going and what I was doing. I decided to turn around, walk back down the block, and stop when I came to a pay phone.

I removed Prodski's card from my wallet and dialed his office number. But all I got was his answering machine. I believe that if he himself had answered I would have gone straight to his office and beaten him to death.

The traitor was extra lucky. He wasn't simply busy or temporarily unavailable but away from the city entirely. He reported, via his tape, that he'd be out of town for the next two weeks and gave the name and number of a colleague in case of a mental emergency. There was room on the tape for a message so I left my name, told him that I was now aware of his stinking betrayal, and proceeded to fill the tape with as many curses as I could think of, using expletives even worse than those I'd used on my mad stroll just a few minutes before.

Emotionally exhausted, I walked along Madison Avenue mumbling to myself. I'd never felt more like an outcast. Even a specialist had given up on me. I now looked with contempt at the people passing by. They were all different—and yet all the same in the way they responded to me. Which was, in essence, not to respond at all. Or at best to give me a quick glance and then dismiss me.

But why should I have expected more?

I slowed my pace because I suddenly felt terribly weak. There'd been no warning this time. The spell seemed to have come out of nowhere. It's happening again, I thought, and as I had done in the past to save myself, I stepped into the street and hailed a cab to speed me home.

My body seemed to calm down a bit once I was settled in my apartment. But my brain would not rest. This time it was determined to go the limit.

AS I STOOD now, months later, just several feet from Jennifer's gallery, stood there as a mental patient on a solo pass, the past returned with force, and seemed so fresh and so inexcusable. All of it was disgustingly vivid. Yet so much of what happened after my meeting with Jennifer was fuzzy in my mind. Perhaps because the days and weeks that followed were uneventful, stagnant. I began to live like a near hermit. I spent hour after hour in my apartment doing nothing but thinking, and trying desperately to sleep without fear. Often I'd fail to remember if it was, say, a Wednesday or a Thursday, if I'd made the morning coffee, gone down for the mail, paid various bills, taken a shower the day before. I blamed those who had abandoned me, tossed me away in disappointment and futility. And as I came to despise them I also came to hate myself, my failures, my oddness.

I suppose I even lost track of when Prodski would return, had become too disoriented and entombed to care about heading outside to confront him. I actually had to force myself to go out for food and I struggled even more to make the weekly trip to the unemployment office. This trip was not only the biggest "social" event of the week, it was the only social event of the week.

I should have known that I couldn't go on this way indefinitely. Because a kind of pressure was building and it was beyond my control.

"I should have gone after him," I told myself now, as I continued to stand right by Jennifer's gallery. Instead of daydreaming about having him beg for mercy, instead of standing before a mirror while pressing the trigger of an empty revolver, I should have made more of an effort to take charge of my mind, and followed through with any readily available thing that could serve as a weapon—a knife, a hammer, a pair of scissors.

I should have left that block then, because just being near Jennifer's gallery, which was in effect being near Jennifer, and in a way near Elizabeth and Prodski as well, was doing damage to my stability, causing my brain to retreat, to relapse. Yet there was something in me that wouldn't let the opportunity pass. It was as if I wanted to aggravate a wound that was only beginning to heal. So I hugged the wall of the building. And then I inched my way to the window of the gallery. A passerby might have thought I was a nut case who fancied himself a spy.

I peeked in briefly, saw nothing but twisted black metal hanging on the wall, then backed my head away from the window to avoid being seen by someone inside the gallery. I allowed a few moments to pass and then peeked again. This time I saw, at the far left side of the gallery, a man in a dark suit talking with Jennifer. She was dressed in a dark suit as well and was her usual lively self, moving her hands about for emphasis as she lectured by one of the junk sculptures for sale.

I was struck again by her resemblance to Elizabeth. And it then dawned on me that Elizabeth, ever since she'd changed jobs, had been emulating Jennifer. Yes, she'd been competing with her sister and trying to top her. In dress, style, manner. Yet retaining her moral superiority. Amazing. And almost, but not quite, amusing.

I kept staring at Jennifer while at the same time wondering what her double was doing at the moment. Well, of course she was at work, but who was she talking to, what plans was she making for the evening, did those plans involve a new companion?

I began to move toward the gallery door, revealing myself completely in the window. I was actually about to enter the gallery and greet Jennifer and then damn her to hell for putting Prodski in my life, but when she briefly glanced my way by accident and then did a double take, I suddenly feared being recognized and took off, as fast as I could, down the block.

I crossed Fifth Avenue and rested on a bench by Central Park. A pigeon landed nearby and then waddled about in front of me, moving back and forth, this way and that, as if he too were in a quandary.

In Essex I'd contained my anger and hoped that it would eventually subside if I left the past behind and concentrated more on the present and future. It's funny how just seeing Jennifer's gallery, along with Jennifer herself, had wrecked all my efforts to reform, had erased days, weeks, months, and made me feel much as I had when I'd retreated to my apartment, taking Jennifer's revelation with me and adding it to my miserable history.

I looked at my watch. It was almost 2:35.

I remembered that it was a Wednesday. And that on Wednesdays Prodski's last patient was at two o'clock. He'd leave the clinic some time after that session ended, at around three, to do some sort of rotten consulting work at a hospital. I'd memorized his schedule. Amazingly, stupidly, I'd been comforted back then by knowing where he'd be during the day.

"I'm going to get him," I announced there by Central Park, with a pigeon as witness. "I going to get him now."

And in firmly making this announcement, I felt committed to act on it.

Hadn't I, after all, been deluding myself? My losses were too great. My life was at an end. I was too tired to rise up and start a new one. And even if I did have the strength, *what* would I be starting? And hadn't all my spells been a way of telling me that my very existence had been a terrible blunder from the very start?

"Do it," I said. "Finish it."

So I hailed a cab and told the driver to go crosstown and then up Broadway into the Nineties. And I told him to make it fast.

I didn't even have to consider this as an act of revenge. One could say that I was a good Samaritan, saving patients from a charlatan, a dangerous meddler, a self-righteous, perverse foreigner who took pleasure in toying with lives.

The traffic was still light at this time of day and so we sped along and reached Broadway in what seemed like minutes. I actually was ahead of schedule.

Once we were in the high Eighties I asked the driver to slow down so I could more clearly see the shops we were passing.

"Stop here," I ordered when one particular store caught my eye. I asked the driver to wait while I purchased an item from the place, called simply Sam's Hardware.

"I can't stay here long," the driver said.

"Won't be a minute," I assured him. "I know what I want."

I asked the man at the counter—possibly Sam himself—for an inexpensive knife, of moderate size, but with a fairly wide blade. He picked one that was some nine inches long. "Ten dollars," he said, and removed the blade from its cardboard sheath. "Nice knife for the price, razor sharp."

I imagined the blade easily penetrating Prodski's chubby back. "I'll take it," I said, paying for it, courtesy of Uncle Arthur, who of course had no idea that he'd be financing a murder. The man slipped the knife back into its sheath and put it in a black plastic bag.

"Okay," I told the driver as I returned to the cab. "Doing some household repairs. Needed a special screwdriver."

These remarks weren't necessary, but I suppose I was feeling guilty about my crime even though I hadn't as yet committed it.

"Yeah, man, I can relate," said the driver, "I got a leaky faucet in the bathroom. Never stops dripping. The super tried to fix the damn thing three or four times already, but all he's good for is taking out the garbage."

As we traveled several blocks into the Nineties, I removed my coat, took the knife from the bag, and draped the coat over the knife.

I had the driver drop me off a block from the clinic.

I realized, of course, that Prodski might very well have changed his schedule since I'd last been in contact with the bastard, but I hoped that luck was on my side.

I approached the clinic from across the street, and as I moved closer, and the red house with its weird lone turret grew larger, I started to get shaky. "I'm going to do it," I said. He deserved it. And yet though I was urging myself on, trying to transform my anger into true homicidal madness, I also couldn't help but wish that Prodski was gone for the day.

Then I saw something that confirmed he was not.

The clinic and the house on the far side of it were separated by a narrow alley, which was just big enough to serve as a parking space for a small car. And because of Prodski's status as head of the clinic, the space was reserved for him and his shiny new red Volkswagen.

That car was now in the alley.

I looked at my watch. It wasn't even three o'clock yet. I'd made remarkable time, even with the stop-off for a murder weapon.

Since I was standing directly across the street from the clinic now and feared being seen, I tried to use one of the trees that lined the street as cover. But it wasn't much help since it was a rather scrawny thing about as thick as a cheap flagpole. So I began to pace, a few feet to my left, then a few to my right, repeatedly consulting my watch, to give the impression to anyone who might consider me suspicious that I was waiting, rather impatiently, for a friend. At the same time I kept a firm grip on the knife under my folded London Fog and kept a steady eye on the clinic's stoop and its very solid oak door.

The sun, which had been out all afternoon, was now lost in a huge bundle of fair-weather clouds, and the air seemed cooler, enough to make me wish that I could put on my coat. I started to tremble and tried to warm myself by again calling up my anger, my rage. But this didn't have much effect and soon my teeth were chattering.

I couldn't tell any more if I was trembling because of the weather or nerves or both combined.

You have to do it, my mind told me. It's the only way to get some relief, some justice.

At times Prodski had used the term *displacement* in our chat sessions. He'd suggested that I'd shifted all sorts of anxieties onto my spells, that I'd created them as a way of giving vent to problems I couldn't or refused to express or face. A lot of nonsense, I thought, psychiatric mumbo jumbo. But as I waited for him to appear at his door, I wondered if I was doing something of the sort in this case. Perhaps in attacking Prodski I'd really be attacking a whole host of other people, other things—my mother and her stifling strength, my father and his awful weakness, my brain and body and the spells they shared, Elizabeth, Jennifer, fellow workers, Lorch, schoolmates, the city, the world, the creator, the madman, whoever, whatever had dreamt up this entire mess. I think Prodski would have appreciated such an astute analysis.

But did it really matter how much or how little Prodski served as a kind of scapegoat? He remained guilty.

The door opened at last. My heart began pounding so hard that the beats reached my ears and seemed to drown out any street sounds.

With my coat still draped over my arm and concealing the knife, I removed the cardboard sheath from the blade and then ducked behind a car. My movements must have looked very bizarre, but I suppose I wasn't even thinking about possible witnesses at this point. I peered over the fender and saw a man in a suit descending the several stone steps that led from the door to the sidewalk.

But the man wasn't Prodski, just some well-dressed colleague or patient.

I stood up as he walked down the street and turned the corner.

I was both relieved and disappointed.

My watch read seven minutes past three.

I had to consider the possibility that Prodski had revised his schedule and was now seeing a three o'clock patient, which meant that I could be in for an hour's wait. I wasn't sure I could hold up for so long. The tension would become unbearable. My body was already in a state and such continuing agitation might very well touch off an attack. Yes, I was—and had been throughout the day—pushing my luck.

The door opened again. And again I ducked down. But this time it was Prodski who was walking down the steps.

There he was, the rat, dressed in a dark-brown corduroy jacket with a black turtleneck, carrying his stupid black leather briefcase, in which he probably kept records of patients he'd eventually destroy with his expert guidance, his notions of facing reality.

I waited until he reached the alley to rise up and cross the street. This time I did survey the area for potential witnesses. Because I'd suddenly realized that I might actually be able to get away with this thing I was about to do. If no one saw me and if I disposed of the knife, say, in the Hudson or even in the Central Park Lake and if I then returned to Essex on schedule, who'd connect me with the murder? Having occurred in an alley, perhaps the killing would be perceived as a mugging gone wrong.

This optimistic little scenario should have calmed me somewhat, but I was shaking all over and my legs had turned to rubber.

I squeezed the handle of the knife, trying to direct all the tension in me to my hand, as I approached the alley and watched Prodski approach his car.

But I stopped. And I just stood there, stood dumbly by the entrance to the alley and watched as Prodski fumbled with his keys, accidentally dropped them, and bent down to pick them up.

I couldn't advance. I just couldn't go through with it.

"All this is crazy, absolutely crazy," I said, as if I'd awakened from a mad dream and found myself on the brink of completing it in real life. From the time I'd left Jennifer's gallery until now, I'd been indulging in a ridiculous and dangerous fantasy.

Had I come to my senses? Was I simply a coward? Or did I really wish to try again, reenter the world and attempt to solidify my presence?

All I knew was that I couldn't force myself to use the knife or to confront Prodski in any way. I couldn't even bring myself to actually enter the alley. I remained frozen at the entrance.

As it turned out, there was no opportunity for second thoughts. Because just then some man came hurrying from the clinic toward me. I immediately turned away from the alley and started to move down the block. At first I imagined that the man had recognized my intentions and was determined to make a kind of citizen's arrest. But then he called out, "Andre! Going my way?!" and I realized that he was probably a colleague of Prodski's who wanted a lift.

Prodski never saw me. And although his colleague might have wondered why I was standing by the alley, he was too preoccupied to make anything of the business.

At first I was just hurrying down the street to the avenue. But then I found myself running—afraid, crazily enough, that Prodski would soon drive by and spot me.

I was out of breath when I turned the corner and had to stop. I wasn't used to running. Or, for that matter, walking about for hours. Except for a few group outings the only exercise I'd gotten while in Essex was making the trip from my room to the dayroom and back several times a day.

The red car was nowhere in sight.

Getting my bearings, I noticed that Prodski's street was one-way, with traffic going east. And I'd been running west. That's why I'd managed to escape. Though considering my complete failure to act, I'd essentially escaped from nothing.

I was about to bend over and rub my aching calves when I realized that I was still holding the knife. This fact seemed to frighten me now, made me feel like a criminal, and I looked around to see if a policeman or patrol car was nearby. I noticed a garbage can by the corner and while keeping an eye out for passersby I casually walked over to the receptacle, removed the knife from under my coat, and allowed it to drop from my hand and join the other trash.

Just then two schoolkids emerged from a little grocery store a few shops away from where I was standing. Almost sure that they'd seen me dispose of the knife, I panicked, crossed the avenue, and once again flagged down a cab.

I DECIDED to take Dr. Petersen's suggestion and visit my apartment. It really had been more than just a mere suggestion. At least, that's the way I'd interpreted it. My dealing with such a visit and overcoming its unpleasant associations were apparently necessary before I could be considered worthy of release. Of course, I could pretend that I'd returned, but for some reason I needed to prove to myself that I could actually do it.

I closed my eyes as we traveled back downtown and tried to relax. Now that I was seated and at rest, I was conscious of my fatigue. Everything hurt—feet, legs, arms, head. Even my eye sockets ached. Coatless as I'd been, I'd caught a chill, so I welcomed the stuffiness and warmth of the cab, didn't even mind its damp, slightly foul odor, which I couldn't identify. As for my nerves, they felt shot, so overtaxed that I wondered if they'd come back to life, and then entertained the hope that they would not.

I was relieved that I was safe, so appreciative that my troubled brain had corrected itself enough to prevent me from following through with an insane plan. I could very well have been a murderer on the loose, but here I was instead, an ordinary, law-obeying citizen returning to his apartment building.

Yet, though I was basically back where I started, back on track with my solo, I was feeling quite frustrated, as if I'd been forced to abandon an essential task, to accept defeat. I imagined Prodski driving to his hospital, chatting with his passenger, humming along to classical music on his car radio, free as a bird, so full of himself and his wisdom, and of course totally unaware of how close he'd come to lying dead in an alley. The thought that he remained alive, active, and untouched in this world would continue to disturb me. He'd be lurking in my brain as usual, seemingly indestructible.

As we entered my neighborhood—which I now thought of as my "old neighborhood," though I'd been absent for only some two months—I became leery about immediately going to the apartment. I hadn't been thinking much about the old place, but now that I was, I wasn't all that anxious to see it. It was a place of the past, a place of exile, and although I had existed in it and tried to make it livable and familiar, I'd always thought of it as a temporary residence—though I'd had no idea where or if I'd ever find a place I could regard as permanent.

Since I'd eaten virtually nothing all day and my stomach was beginning to growl, I told the driver to drop me off by my local coffee shop on Broadway. Yes, it was a way of avoiding my apartment for a while but it also was a practical decision, for as far as I knew there was no food left in my refrigerator. I'm sure that if I'd told Uncle Arthur that I planned to visit my apartment, he would have gone typically overboard and filled the shelves. But I'd purposely kept my intentions from him. I didn't want him interfering with my visit in any way.

As I was stepping out of the cab, I happened to glance up at the old discolored blue sign above the coffee shop. The name, in dirty white letters, seemed familiar enough, THE OLYMPIA. But I could have sworn that I'd never seen the dirty white image of the Acropolis that was next to it. This oversight or possible lapse of memory disturbed me, made me feel disoriented.

The inside of the shop had that same familiar yet unfamiliar appearance. I'd been in the place many times before, but I didn't recall it being so brightly, harshly lit and I was almost certain that the plastic seats had been dark brown and not their current deep red. I thought at first that the seats might have been redone during my absence, but then noticed that all the plastic had a worn look about it and that some of the seats, particularly those in the booths, had been patched with tape.

Where's my mind going? I wondered, smiling to myself and dismissing these observations as nonsense. They, unfortunately, lingered on and probably contributed to the very unexpected problem that would soon arise.

The Olympia seemed surprisingly crowded for late afternoon, but as I looked around more carefully I remembered Uncle Arthur and his friends and realized that all the senior citizens who now filled the place were there for the early bird specials. The rest of the crowd was made up of younger customers—clusters of noisy schoolkids and several aspiring actor and actress types in deep conversation, probably about lost jobs. The shop was so packed that a few of the nonancient set were resigned to standing by the register as they waited for a free booth.

When I noticed a man, dressed as a security guard, leave his seat at the counter, I quickly took possession of it. And I was ridiculously proud that I'd secured it, as if I'd won a significant competition.

But this feeling didn't last long. For as I sat there, squeezed between a heavyset middle-aged woman and a very husky, very large young man dressed as a janitor or repairman and intent on sharing his chunky legs and general bulk with those next to him, I began to feel uncomfortable and claustrophobic and my appetite began to weaken. Smoke rose up from the open grill. Smoke rose up from the coffee machine. And all of it seemed to be drifting over to me.

Maybe it was because of the stale air or the heat of the crowd and of the place itself or my aches and pains and a developing headache, but I was now feeling rather nervous. When the gruff, harried man behind the counter asked for my order I was no longer very hungry at all. More to please him than myself, I asked for a cup of coffee and a plain donut. Despite my deteriorating condition, it was still nice to be able to order something again, to be in command, to be served as a normal human being. It was nice to be trusted with a real knife instead of a piece of plastic. And I looked forward to not having to eat off a tray.

But when my coffee came and I added milk to it I couldn't keep my hand steady and some of the milk spilled into the saucer, creating a little white pond.

I couldn't understand why my nervousness was growing rather than subsiding. By now I should have been acclimated to the shop and its deficiencies. And although I had taken a wrong solo turn earlier, I was more or less thinking sanely again. Yet instead of feeling relaxed and relieved and free, I felt tense and somewhat trapped.

As for the heat that filled the shop, I could have lessened its effect by simply removing my jacket. But if I was embarrassed by my loosely fitting jacket, I was even more

ashamed of my dress shirt, which seemed to be swim-
ming on me, and I chose not to reveal it. For some reason I
needed to maintain a certain dignity, even in the Olympia.

Someone was suddenly talking to me. It was the woman
to my right. "What?" I said. "Could you pass the sugar?"
she asked. In passing the sugar, I almost knocked over the
creamer. "Thanks, dear," she said. And I managed a smile,
though my lips were quivering.

Sweat started to drip from my face onto my shirt and
jacket. It gave me a start. Because it was colored sweat.
Sweat with something in it. I didn't understand at first. But
then I recalled the talcum powder I'd rubbed into my skin
to hide my beard. Apparently I was sweating it off. So I
quickly patted my face with my napkin. "What kind of
donut you say?" the man behind the counter asked with a
funny accent. But I was so concerned about my condition
that I couldn't recall my order. This seemed to aggravate
him and he looked at me as if I were moron. "What kind?"
he repeated. "Plain, glaze-ed, sugar, what?" "Plain," I said,
afraid to tell him that I'd changed my mind and now
wanted nothing. "All we got is a glaze-ed left." "Anything,"
I said abruptly, wondering if my pats had removed too
much talcum and left weird clean spots on my face. "You
okay?" asked the man. "You don't look so good." "Fine," I
said, "a little hot maybe." I think I'm suffering, I wanted to
tell him, or anyone. I think I'm in trouble.

I turned away from his eyes and the eyes of a fellow
counterman, whom he mumbled something to. And when

I turned that's when I noticed it. Just above the glass case where they kept cakes, pies, and pudding was a curved metal mirror. In it you could see most of the counter and part of the rest of the shop. And there I was in the curved, crowded scene. There I was with all these people, all these strangers. I should have been terribly pleased. For I was back again. Functional again. Trying to mingle again. Yet I found the sight sickening, with the mirror seeming to capture the way I was now feeling—vague, ugly, alien.

What am I doing here? I thought. Why am I exposing myself in this way?

For the first time during this day I was truly aware of how far I had come. And of the risk I'd been taking. It was me in the shop. Me on the outside. Alone. Away.

I couldn't quite believe it was happening. Because I'd been so steady throughout my solo, traveling about distant streets, courageously exploring new spaces. I'd even been composed enough to plan and nearly commit a murder. And here I was, for God's sake, only a block from my apartment. But as I continued to sweat and my heart became overactive and my skin turned soft and pasty, and the shop and its people appeared increasingly strange, I couldn't deny that an attack was coming and that it had real strength and that unless I acted in some way to nip it in the bud it would cause my collapse.

The only solution was to leave the Olympia immediately and get to the nearest familiar, solitary place where I could possibly calm myself. There wasn't much of a choice in the matter. My apartment was that place. And I had to get there before the attack hit with full force.

As I reached into my left jacket pocket for my wallet, I felt an odd solid bulge in my right. I lifted the object out and saw that it was a copy of *The War of the Worlds.* I'd pretty much forgotten about it, forgotten about my crime. "Madness," I said, staring down at the book, which I had absolutely no desire to read or possess, and which now struck me as further evidence of a still unsettled, unreliable mind.

I had nothing smaller than a ten-dollar bill and just couldn't wait for change, so I left the whole thing on the counter and hurried for the door. "Hey," the woman at the register called out to me angrily, "what about your check?!" "I paid!" I shouted back. "Triple the price!"

The block separating me from my apartment building was long and steep. It was lined with shops of various kinds, so I knew that if things got critical and I felt that I was losing myself completely I could enter one and ask for help. While this seemed like a comforting emergency plan, I knew deep down that I would never take advantage of it. I'd be far too ashamed to reveal my problem, and would rather evaporate on the sidewalk than have a stranger stand by in his place of business and witness my weakness and terror and dissolution.

I tried to pace myself as I climbed the hill. The day had already exhausted me and if I attempted to walk too fast at this point I'd only put more pressure on my failing body and fall apart by the time I reached halfway up the block. The confused nature of my spells continued to puzzle me. At times I would feel a strong need to disappear, actually want to fade and thus escape. But when I'd sense that this was possible, feel my body leaving, I'd panic and pray for a reversal. Then I'd be caught, struggling between this world and the unknown, between something and nothing. And it would be torture.

As people passed me, some walking up the hill, others coming down, I wondered if they were aware, even remotely, of my distress. I had to assume that I didn't matter, and probably would continue not to matter unless I did something outrageous. Little did they know that this seemingly innocuous man in their midst might soon have the urge to scream and keep on screaming.

There was something odd about the shops along the block. They weren't in the order that I remembered them. The drugstore was where the pizza shop should have been and the Chinese restaurant should have followed the shoemaker's rather than vice versa. The jumble confused my brain, added to the headache that had begun in the Olympia. And it got me to wonder about my relationship to the neighborhood as a whole. I couldn't have cared for the place very much or have belonged to it, even in a tentative way, if I couldn't properly recall the layout of a central street, one that I'd frequently walked and shopped on.

Despite the headache, the muddled thoughts, and a bit of dizziness that always seemed to precede a spell, I'd succeeded in climbing about one-third of the block without the spell overtaking me. I kept reminding myself that my apartment building was ridiculously close by and my anxiety was therefore unwarranted. But that old business of being so near and yet so far seemed all too true.

I could sense myself losing ground. Whatever strength was left in my legs was apparently fading. My arms were going limp. My whole body was clammy and sick, as if it had suddenly been invaded by a powerful strain of flu.

I must have looked drunk as I stumbled on, particularly when the dizziness became so severe that I had to find a section of brick wall between shops to lean against in an attempt to rest and allow the symptoms, which were rushing in and then out, like waves, to keep away long enough for me to continue on and reach my destination.

Each time I left a section of wall and tried to walk without support, I feared that I'd float away because my body had lost virtually all of its substance. "Hey, mister," someone called out, "you're dragging your coat." And indeed I'd been holding my London Fog so carelessly that one of its sleeves had been wiping the sidewalk. The story of my life, I thought as I struggled like an uncoordinated fool to fold it more effectively, people care more about my coat than me.

I still couldn't believe that after having spent such a successful day in another and totally different neighborhood, I was experiencing an attack one block from my own building. "This isn't fair," I protested. I deserved to be rewarded, not punished once again.

I'd probably gone wrong in being so active after weeks of confinement. I'd put too much of a strain on myself. Fatigue had weakened any resistance I might have built up against attacks. But, then again, perhaps a message was being sent to me via a major spell—to move on, to settle elsewhere, to leave this area for good.

The spell took a particularly cruel turn. Its force was like nothing I'd ever known. Sweat poured down my face in a seemingly endless flow. My heart was beating so fast it couldn't seem to catch up with itself. I could feel it like never before, sense its shape and interior. And its heightened, mad activity was causing real pain in my chest.

I was losing all control of my body. I thought of a marionette whose strings are cut all at once, its arms, legs, head collapsing. My body had nearly become that useless. And I felt that I was shrinking. I'd soon be the size of a child, then a baby, then a fetus.

As a last resort, I struck one of the brick walls with my fist, badly bruising my knuckles. But still the spell persisted.

"This is impossible," I said. "One block. Damn it all. One block!"

Little black spots then appeared in my eyes and started to accumulate and obscure my vision. My shirt was soaked with perspiration and a passing breeze had managed to reach the wet material and chill it. Now though my throbbing head was red hot, my body was cold.

I knew that I was seconds away from passing out and being carried off.

But I refused to be done in, even with the ground giving way under me, the street rapidly darkening. And so, out of habit, I rushed into the street and looked for a cab. It seemed absurd to take one for little more than half a block, but this was no time to worry about appearances and convention. I had to save myself.

Two cabs approached but they were occupied. With my body beginning to dissolve, my eyesight failing, my brain shutting down, I just didn't have the patience or courage to wait a second longer. So I rushed back to the sidewalk and began running up the block. I could hardly feel my legs anymore and wasn't sure if my feet were actually connecting with the pavement, but I seemed to be advancing nonetheless and that was all that mattered. It was almost as if I were trying to outrun the spell, to leave it behind me. But it maintained its strength and each time it was on the verge of taking me down completely, I was forced to stop, catch my breath, and hope for enough of a quick recovery to push on.

I could see my building in the distance. Just a quarter of a block to go, then across the avenue, past the corner house, and there it was. I imagined myself in my apartment, collapsing in my easy chair. The attack that was so horribly debilitating would then become just a memory. I'm going to make it, I thought, as I paused for a breath. It'll all be over soon. I'm going to survive. And I continued to run, seemingly propelled by an outside force, as if a magical wind were carrying my hopelessly frail, featherlike body forward. I could have been dreaming or so ill and feverish that I'd become delirious.

The traffic light at the corner had just turned red, but with the afternoon sun now conspiring with the spell to beat me down, to finish me off, I couldn't wait for it to change. So I dashed into traffic, barely skirting some vehicles, and relying on others to simply slow down or cut around me. As I reached the corner, several drivers cursed me violently. "You fuckin' nut!" one of them yelled, loud enough to wake the dead.

But I didn't care what any of them said. I was steps away from my building, and it looked as if I'd once again been granted more time in this world.

PART IV

ALL MY SYMPTOMS started to fade once I was inside my building. It was as if a terminal illness had suddenly gone into rapid, miraculous remission. Yet the spell had taken its toll. My whole body was still shaking. And I couldn't remember which of my keys unlocked the lobby door and had to fumble about with spastic hands before I found the right one.

Perhaps my memory was indeed failing me because everything about the building appeared somewhat off. The lobby walls, as I remembered them, were painted white, but here they were a very pale, watery yellow. And I recalled the lobby itself as being larger and less narrow. The mailboxes should have been, according to my brain, a dirty gold, but were instead a dull silver.

As I waited for the elevator, leaning against the wall in my sweat-soaked shirt, suit, and underwear, I could hear the familiar groan of the elevator as it descended. But I could also hear, and feel, a completely new sound. There was a strange rumbling in the lobby floor. I assumed that it was coming from the basement, perhaps from the boiler room. I had a hard time believing that it had always been present and that I just hadn't noticed it before. But if this were the case then I was glad that I hadn't, for the noise was unsettling and threatening and made you fear an explosion that would blast the lobby and you to pieces.

The elevator was also smaller than I recalled, allowing room for only four passengers at most. And hadn't there been a mirror above the button panel?

My apartment door was just as I remembered it, an ugly dark-brown metal slab, with three locks—one in the knob itself and two independent locks above. That there were no surprises here comforted me. But when I had to select the proper key for the proper lock, I couldn't make an immediate match and had to proceed by trial and error. "Come on, come on," I said in frustration. I was too wasted to have to play games on top of everything else I'd endured.

When I finally managed to unlock all the locks, I confidently turned the knob. But the door wouldn't open. Apparently in my confused state I'd forgotten which way to turn a key and had relocked one of the locks. "Damn it," I said, "damn it all," because if this anxiety-provoking nonsense continued it could stimulate an attack in my own hallway. So I forced my weakened mind to focus hard on the task and after a few more tries I succeeded in gaining entrance. "About time," I said.

Though all the blinds were open, the apartment was, as usual, dim and shadowy. As I entered the living room and located my easy chair, I glanced briefly out the window to see the brick walls of surrounding buildings—inhibitors of light, backdrops for depression. I was rather amazed that I'd been able to exist in such a grim atmosphere for so long. Because it almost immediately added to my troubled state.

I sprawled out on the mock leather chair, resting my legs on the accompanying stool, closed my eyes, and allowed my exhausted body to recover. I felt tremendously lucky for having lived through such an overwhelming spell—surely one of the worst I'd ever had. But that the spell had occurred now, with me feeling so confident and relatively normal and so close to achieving release, was very disturbing, very discouraging. I wondered if I'd been fooling myself all along, just pretending that I'd achieved significant control of my mind and body.

Although the weather had turned somewhat cooler, the day was still relatively mild. Nonetheless, the apartment felt quite cold and uncomfortable and seemed to grow even colder as the time passed.

Unable to tolerate my wet, sticky clothes any longer, I got up with the intention of changing my entire outfit. But when I began turning on lamps and light fixtures through-out the apartment to better see what I was doing, I was shocked by the look of the place.

I'd been a failure as a housekeeper and had allowed the apartment to go to seed. But somehow I'd grown accus-tomed to its wrecked appearance, its clutter and dust, even thought that such neglect gave the dreary dump a bit of character and a certain homey, lived-in quality. Perhaps I also was, in a way, getting back at my mother, who'd al-ways kept our home so neat and tidy and sterile.

The apartment I gazed upon now reminded me of her obsessive cleanliness and sense of order. The cheap, non-descript furniture, much of which had come with the apartment and had been dust collectors, was now so highly polished that it gleamed. Some surfaces even reflected in a mirrorlike way any nearby lightbulb. If you got close enough to an individual piece—an end table, chest of drawers, coffee table—you could detect a rather disgusting lemon scent. Even the bookshelf and the books themselves gave off that odor.

The bluish-gray living room rug, which had always been spotted with lint and looked rather old and worn, now appeared fresh, as if someone had gone over it vigor-ously and repeatedly with a vacuum and had possibly given it a scrubbing as well.

And—as if my mind hadn't been plagued enough by unreliable memories—I now had to deal with an apart-ment in which a good part of the furniture had been rearranged. This was particularly obvious in the living room, where the couch had been moved from the wall to the middle of the room, and chairs, which had been perfectly fine in their various corners, had been placed directly opposite the couch, with the coffee table serving as a kind of centerpiece. One of these chairs was my easy chair, and I now understood why it hadn't felt quite right when I'd collapsed in it.

As I surveyed the overly neat, lifeless room, I also noticed things that hadn't been there before, things brought in by someone else. There were framed prints on the wall that looked like images you might find on greeting cards—a cute little cottage covered with vines and surrounded by flowers, a lighthouse emitting a courageous, spiritual light as huge waves struck the base of the tower, a deer pausing by a forest stream, with a hint of mountains in the background. On the coffee table was a crystal candy dish filled with hard candy and a metallic vase holding several plastic white roses. My modest TV set was still on its movable stand, but the stand had been placed in a corner—temporarily it seemed, as if the phantom decorator hadn't yet fitted it into his redesign scheme.

"What in God's name have you done?" I said.

The person I was addressing, and felt like cursing, was of course Uncle Arthur.

This time he'd gone too far with his kindness and concern. In an effort to make my eventual homecoming pleasant and to somewhat free my apartment from the past, he'd turned the place into a kind of no-man's-land. It was neither my place nor his, but rather an uneasy mixture of the two. It now felt even less like a home—my home—than it had before. And in altering so much, Uncle Arthur had actually defeated his purpose. Because instead of making me forget what had happened here, the changes caused me to remember what was missing and why those things were gone.

Take the big mirror in the bedroom. The one I'd faced with my empty gun. It'd been replaced by a thinner, cheaper sort, with a simple cheap gold frame. As I looked at it and rejected it, I recalled how I'd grown angry before the old one, incensed by the person reflected in it, and also by the maddening sounds from other apartments that were invading the room—voices, TVs, music. "Shut up!" I'd kept shouting to these noisemakers, these persistent irritants who gave me no peace.

And I'd told the reflection in the mirror, a haggard, miserable creature: "You're not me, you're not me at all." Unable to stand the noise and the reflection and my inability to do away with them, I'd picked up a table lamp and thrown it against the mirror, smashing it to pieces, and then almost wept because I'd destroyed it. And in my despair and in an attempt to further relieve all the tension and anger that was in me, I'd picked up one of the pieces and used it to make cuts in my arm. But once I'd seen the blood and was fully aware of what I had done, my anger got the better of me again and I went about the apartment looking for things to tear apart and destroy. Where's the rotten spell now, when I need it? I'd thought as I stormed through the rooms, shattering, punching, and smashing objects and possessions that no longer seemed to have anything to do with me. Take me now, I remembered saying. Take me.

This visit was supposed to be cathartic, but these memories were becoming too much for me, and I thought it best that I leave the apartment before my solo turned into a nightmare. I'd had more than enough for one day. Why torment myself further? And besides, the cold in the apartment was getting to me.

But I felt cowardly about giving up so soon. After all, this place had no real power over me. It was my mind that had made it significant, given it life, allowed it to take control.

So I decided to remain and change my clothes as I'd intended. Aside from making me more comfortable, the change would, I realized, serve as a kind of proof back on the ward. By appearing in a different outfit from the one I'd been wearing when I'd left, I'd pretty much show Dr. Petersen that I had indeed returned to my apartment and that all had gone well.

When I opened my bedroom closet, I expected the usual huge mess, but instead found clothes neatly hung and carefully spaced. Uncle Arthur strikes again, I thought. There was something crazy about his passion for order and organization. Violating his methods I just threw my wet clothes into the closet as I took them off. I then replaced them with more casual attire—chinos, a dark-blue shirt, and a three-quarter casual coat to be worn when I was outside.

As I was buttoning the last few buttons of the shirt, I noticed a small discolored area on the antique-white wall, just a foot or so away from the cheap new mirror. Obviously Uncle Arthur had missed cleaning it or else had tried to clean it and failed.

I couldn't immediately identify it, but then realized that I might have made it when I'd started punching the wall to protest the loud conversation going on next door. "Shut up!" I'd shouted. "I don't want to hear you! Are you deaf!" And I recalled how I continued to shout and then resorted to throwing whatever was handy at the wall—a book, lightbulb, vase. And I recalled how I couldn't stop my attack once I'd begun, and how some time later people were banging on my front door and ringing my bell and shouting. "Open up! It's the police! Open up!"

Feeling slightly sick again, I went into the bathroom and washed my face with cold water. I wiped myself off with what appeared to be a new, unused towel. Certainly I had never bought one that was dark green with a leaf design running through it. But, of course, Uncle Arthur had. The man must have spent a small fortune on all these items, even if he'd shopped in his usual bargain stores. And while I should have appreciated his thoughtfulness, I was now coming to hate it. For without meaning to he had pretty much succeeded in dispossessing me.

I noticed a crack in the mirror of the medicine cabinet. Nothing major. Just a small crack in the lower right corner. I wondered if I had caused it. Maybe I'd punched the mirror or slammed shut the cabinet door so hard that it had cracked. I couldn't remember for sure, and this bothered me. I stared at the puzzled face in the mirror and despised it for looking so concerned and weak.

I was about to leave the bathroom and the apartment itself when I recalled that I had a bottle of Valium in the medicine cabinet.

Once again I opened a door behind which I expected to be confronted by chaos, only to find everything within beautifully arranged. Here bottles, tubes, blades, Band-Aids had been lined up in a visually pleasing way, with almost artistic care.

The man is mad, I thought. A good Samaritan who'd gone off the deep end.

Luckily, several tablets remained in the bottle. I wasn't sure if Valium mixed well with the other medication I had in my system, but considering the variety of drugs they'd tested on me during my early days in Essex and how well I'd survived them, I assumed there was absolutely no risk in this case. So I swallowed one pill. And then took another. I thought that I might as well return to the ward looking contented and relaxed—further evidence for Dr. Petersen of just how well adjusted I'd become.

I went into the living room, sat in my easy chair, and waited for the drug to take effect. Elizabeth had introduced me to wine, but I wasn't much of a drinker and would get rather tipsy after just a glass or two. That's somewhat the effect that Valium would have on me, before overuse reduced its potency—it'd soften me and make me feel relatively carefree. I suppose I was anticipating that effect now, since I hadn't taken the drug in months.

While waiting, I got a bit bored and so I wheeled the TV over to my chair. I had nearly an hour left to my solo and therefore could safely indulge in a little leisurely entertainment.

But although it was nice to see something on TV other than dopey programs selected by Wally Weston, there was nothing on that really interested me. After flipping through dozens of channels, I paused at a news program that was anchored by a beautiful blond woman in a yellow suit and red paisley scarf. I appreciated her looks, but her robotic voice annoyed me. When she began showing scenes of mutilated bodies on a road outside some devastated desert town, the contrast between her elegance and the horrors to which she so coolly responded struck me as absurd and I wondered if she was a bit drugged up or else somewhat mental. I pressed the mute button to silence her—which reminded me of how an unruly ward patient would be locked in the so-called Quiet Room until he or she became somewhat sensible again. I smiled briefly at the weird comparison, then switched off the set and pushed it away in disgust.

I happened to focus on my desk in the far corner of the room. There was a neat pile of paper on one side of my computer and an equally neat pile of envelopes on the other. Again, Arthur's handiwork. As I crossed the room to get a closer look, I felt slightly dizzy—pleasantly so. The Valium apparently was taking effect. It seemed very minimal, all too minimal in fact, but I had to settle for anything I got.

The envelopes turned out to be junk mail Uncle Arthur had saved for me. All "important" mail he'd religiously brought to the hospital. The pile of paper—the pages so carefully stacked that they formed a solid block—was actually a manuscript I'd been editing before I was fired. *Philosophy and Religion in the Age of the Renaissance*. One of the volumes in the History of Humanity series.

I flipped through the manuscript. About a quarter of it had been worked on—penciled corrections and notes littered the pages. Though I'd apparently made them, they puzzled me now. The grammatical changes, as far as I could interpret them, didn't seem very necessary. As for the scribbled marginal notes, I couldn't really make sense of them. Of course to understand such queries and comments I needed to understand the text, and as I read along I didn't recognize the material. I had forgotten all of it, felt that I was reading it for the first time.

I made an effort to appreciate bits and pieces of text, but the information they contained came across as unimportant—who really cared about all this Renaissance nonsense? What did the Renaissance have to do with me? Or with anything?

"Trivia," I remarked.

Angered by my inability to remember the material and also by the thought that I'd spent much of my adult life working on similar stuff, I grabbed some of the pages and tore them in half, and then in half again, and still again, letting the pieces fall onto Uncle Arthur's beautifully restored carpet.

I suddenly felt like crying.

"I have to get out of here," I said. This place was doing damage to my brain.

So strange. Such a turnabout. For I'd spent so many sleepless nights in this apartment, afraid that a spell would carry me off. And now I was eager to leave it.

I put on my casual coat, and as was my habit, checked the pockets of the coat I'd worn earlier for loose change, a handkerchief, whatever.

I grabbed hold of some sort of metal tube sunk down in the right-hand pocket of the London Fog. "What the——" I began to say, but stopped when I opened my hand and found Parisian Ruby Red. I'd forgotten about Mandy's lipstick and was delighted that it hadn't slipped out of this coat that had been through so much, including a near murder. The lipstick would be my one memento of the outside. I decided not to take along *The War of the Worlds*, the other souvenir—it was, after all, stolen merchandise, evidence of a crime.

"GOOD RIDDANCE," I said to the apartment as I left it behind.

Standing in the elevator, I sensed that the Valium was already wearing off because I was beginning to feel a bit jittery again. By the time the car reached the lobby, which it did in a matter of seconds, I was definitely on edge.

As I headed for the lobby door, I encountered Miss Tice, who was just entering the building with her tiny terrier. The thing looked like an agitated feather duster and its nervousness seemed to heighten my own.

"Any hot water yet?" Miss Tice asked.

I was hardly in the mood to talk and felt that I might collapse if I stood in one spot too long. Yet I couldn't bring myself to be discourteous. Besides, she was blocking the door.

"I'm sorry," I said, "but I don't quite understand the question."

"Didn't you use any water today? We got no hot water again. How in hell are people supposed to take a bath or wash their dishes?"

"I suppose I didn't notice," I said, trying to move around her and the dog, who was sniffing my shoes. "Have you asked Juan?"

"Who the hell is *Juan*?"

I couldn't remember the name of the super, but vaguely recalled that it was Spanish and began with a *J*. Perhaps it was *Jesús*.

"Well, whoever," I said.

"You mean José—I want nothing to do with that useless son of a bitch. He gets insulted every time I complain to the landlord. And you know what he does to get back at me? The bastard goes down to the basement and bangs on the pipes right under my apartment. Sounds like a goddamn brass band. Drives the dog nuts, the poor little thing. But I'm gonna take care of that son-a-bitch someday. He doesn't know who he's dealing with."

I managed to maneuver myself around her and at last had my hand on the door. "Have to be going," I said. "Maybe the hot water is back on now."

"Don't hold your breath. Hey, you're Brunner, right? From the fourth floor. Or Williamson. Which is it?"

"Ott," I answered. "I'm on three."

"What's your name again?"

"Ott. O-t-t."

"That's all of it?"

"That's all there is."

"Sounds like there should be more. Like it's half of something. What the hell kind of name is that? Ott. What is it—German?"

Weakness was overtaking me again, I just couldn't remain in place any longer, and also had no desire to chat with a fellow tenant who didn't even know who I was. So I gave her an abrupt and stupid "Have a nice day," pushed open the door, and left.

I considered taking a bus back to the hospital. The stop was, after all, just across the street on the avenue and the bus would leave me within a block or so from Essex. But traffic seemed to be building up at this time of day and I was feeling fatigued and strange and susceptible and wasn't sure how I'd hold up in a slow-moving and possibly crowded bus. So once again I decided to waste Uncle

Arthur's money on a cab. The meter still had the effect of startling me a bit, registering as it did $2.50, plus a $1.50 surcharge, even before the cab had advanced one block. But I had to be grateful that the service existed. I could rely on cabs if a spell became too overwhelming and I felt the need to immediately flee to a safe place. Needless to say, I always dreaded the possibility of a cab strike.

I tried, once again during this up-and-down day, to rest and regain my strength. I was still very tense, but the closer the cab got to the hospital the more my anxiety decreased. This effect made me realize something I hadn't even thought about before: throughout my stay at Essex I hadn't suffered one attack. Not one. I hadn't even feared that one was on the way. And though I still wasn't particularly close to the people around me—except perhaps for Mandy—none of them seemed like strangers.

When the cab got into heavy traffic and was forced to move very slowly, I distracted myself by concentrating on people walking the streets.

I didn't have much respect for them. They went about with too much ease, functioned too well, oblivious to everything that could go wrong. They didn't have our difficulties. But someday at least a few of them might. For now, however, they all remained children. They hadn't been tested. They knew nothing. Their little individual worlds weren't truly real. They were so inexperienced. They didn't even know that a potential murderer had been among them for an entire afternoon.

And the doctors who came from their ranks were no better. Just look at how I had fooled them. And I would continue to fool them, returning to Essex as an apparently supersuccessful soloist. Because only I had knowledge of my day and I'd tell them just the good parts. That I had this power to deceive pleased me, and I imagined that using this power more fully might make the rest of my stay oddly entertaining.

Despite the problems that arose, I didn't regret my solo. Although I'd experienced certain traumas, I was proud, quite proud, that I'd withstood them.

As we approached Essex I would have felt very content with myself were it not for one thing that continued to weigh on my brain—Prodski remained untouched.

I don't know how the idea came to me. But it came just then. It simply sprang to mind, rather miraculously. Brains are certainly funny and unpredictable. They can take you on a path of destruction, but then suddenly become helpful. And I was delighted that the idea—a kind of plan, you might say—had come just as I was feeling somewhat defeated. And although it seemed rather cruel, I knew that I had to take advantage of it.

Excited by the prospect, I accidentally left the driver a ridiculously generous tip, telling him simply to keep the change. I realized the mistake too late. Since he was so appreciative, I didn't have the nerve to ask for money back. "Have a good one," he said.

"Yes," I said, smiling, "I think I will."

Though feeling very drained, I was completely at ease now that I was right by the hospital. I checked my watch and saw that I had enough time to get to work on the plan. I could have waited, of course—it wasn't as if the plan needed to be acted upon immediately. But I was very pleased about it at this moment, and was afraid that my enthusiasm might lessen in the hours and days ahead. So instead of returning a bit early to the ward, I chose to push my solo to the limit and remain outside.

I walked three blocks to an old candy store we'd stopped at on group walks. I remembered how the little foreign man who worked there would eye the group with suspicion. He didn't recognize me now as I bought a mechanical pencil and a pad of letter-size white paper. Which only goes to show that if you don't look or act crazy and are not in the company of madmen, you'll be regarded as normal and treated respectfully. It's all a matter of playing the part well.

Not far from the shop was a sad and very narrow vest-pocket park, which, wedged as it was between two buildings, probably had been just an empty lot once upon a time. It was visited mainly by bums, but on one of our group walks we'd used it as a resting place. Although there was a real chill in the air and a rather strong breeze, I decided to sit down for a while and work on my drawing. Except for a stray bum hunched over a far bench, the park was appealingly empty.

I hadn't really fooled with caricatures since my youth, when I would grow tired from reading and entertain myself by drawing stupid cartoonlike heads, some based on real people, others merely imaginary. I wasn't all that good, but I did have some talent, which was better than having none whatsoever. Yet I'd always considered it a rather worthless talent, just a step above doodling. Always, that is, until now.

Since I was so long out of practice, I had to make a dozen or so sketches before the results started to please me. When I was finally satisfied that I had captured the general shape of his face and the cut of his hair, had come close at least to the look of his eyes, nose, and lips, then I began to erase a few lines here, a few lines there, expanding or reducing them, correcting, refining, until the dopey portrait approximated the real-life subject.

His chubby cheeks and slight double chin were easy enough to render, but his characteristic self-satisfied smile gave me trouble. It was hard to convey that sort of subtlety in a cartoon drawing. But for my purposes I thought the picture was suggestive enough, and what with the other information I'd provide it would serve as a helpful guide.

As I was putting the finishing touches on the sketch, a little kid, who was walking by the park with his mother, broke away from her and ran up to me. "Whataya drawing, mister?" he said.

"Hugo!" his mother yelled. "Come back here. Leave that man alone."

"Could I see?" asked the boy, ignoring his mother's commands.

That's it, I wanted to tell him. Don't let her intimidate you. The more independent you are, the better. It'll save you a lot of grief in the future.

But I showed him the picture instead.

"He's funny," said the kid. "Who is he?"

"A monster," I told him, just as his mother grabbed him by the coat and pulled him away.

I wrote the name of the funny monster under his picture. But my handwriting wasn't quite legible and I decided to erase it and print the letters instead. I also made them larger.

P-R-O-D-S-K-I

Actually, in terms of the plan, it was a lot more important that the address of his clinic could be easily read, and so I printed it with great care. Under it I noted his schedule as best as I could remember it.

As I was doing all of this, I again thought about the plan itself. Yes, it was cruel. But I wondered if it also was rather cowardly.

I concluded that you sometimes have to make a sacrifice, but that you don't necessarily have to sacrifice yourself. As for being a coward—hadn't I proven myself time and again? I'd faced loneliness, abuse, betrayal, breakdown, and of course spell after spell. The very fact that I was still here, in this world, was evidence of my resilience, my bravery. Other unlucky souls had not fared so well. And rehabilitation or resurrection seemed unlikely. I suppose I believed that I could succeed whereas they could not. For despite my spells and my problems with this world, I was choosing to stay and struggle on and find an adequate place.

Before I risked questioning my conclusions, seeing them as excuses, bits of pomposity, and feeling pangs of guilt, I hurried back to Essex to put the plan in motion.

"VISITOR?" ASKED THE guard at the security desk.

"Patient," I answered, handing him my solo pass. "Ward 13." I was rather glad to give this identity. Even announced it quite loudly. My lack of embarrassment surprised me. I sounded, in fact, almost proud of my status.

The young nurse Bobbie answered my knock on the ward door. She smiled at me as I entered. "How'd it go?" she asked. "Fine," I said. "Beautiful day out," she said. "Yes, very," I said, "though it's getting a bit chilly." "Is it? Well, it's that time of year, I guess." "Indeed."

I believe I sounded, during this little exchange of idle chitchat, as stable as anyone could. There wasn't even a hint in my voice or manner of what I'd been through or how close I'd come to disaster. I'd recovered beautifully— though none of the staff would even suspect that I had *recovered* from anything.

I removed my coat and walked to my room. My body still retained some of the chill of the outside and I welcomed the pleasant warmth that filled the ward. It felt— what is that expression people use? Oh, yes. *Comfy.* That's the way it felt. Comfy.

Carl wasn't in the room, which I must admit didn't bother me in the least. Of late he'd become more of a burden than a comfort. After I hung up my coat in the closet, I paused for a few moments to look about the room. When I'd first entered it weeks ago, it had seemed cold and uninviting, a cross between a motel room and an institutional space. But now it appeared more appealing than the apartment I'd just left. It was neat, simply decorated. The bedspreads matched the bluish rug and curtains. The chest of drawers was squat and unobtrusive rather than overbearing. The little wooden desk by the window was rather charming. And, of course, the little panes of glass continued to recall an English cottage. In short, the room felt rather—rather comfy. And sort of "cozy" as well.

I removed my Prodski sketch from the side pocket of the coat. Before I'd entered the hospital I'd simply torn it off the pad, folded it a couple of times, pocketed it, and then thrown the pad itself into a trash basket on the corner. I had to consider future developments, the possible execution and success of the plan. No sense, I thought, in taking the chance of someone finding that pad in my possession and then linking the sketch to me.

As I approached Tommy Leon's room, I was grateful that the hallway was empty. Though even if someone on staff did see us talking, they would hardly regard it as suspicious. Tommy, after all, spoke to anyone who bothered to listen.

He was sitting on the floor, leaning over a large sheet of drawing paper, probably gotten from Miss Holly, the occupational therapist. Positioned as he was, he looked like a child entertaining himself. When he saw me in the doorway, he immediately picked up his drawing and came over.

"This is my attack plan for Cuba," he said, proudly holding up the mad thing, filled with his usual violent scribbles. He then went on to detail his plan for "killing all the fucks."

"Sounds good," I said, to humor him.

I checked the hallway to make sure no one was observing us, and then I surprised him by unfolding my sketch. I held it close to my body as if it were a secret document meant for his eyes only. I thought his brain would appreciate this clandestine routine.

I told him that this was the doctor who'd committed him to Courtland months ago. That this was, roughly, what he looked like. And that this was his name, the address of his clinic, and a fairly accurate record of his schedule.

"How'd you find out?" he asked. He was all fired up. In fact, he was so excited and angry that I was afraid he might grab the sheet from my hands and mutilate it.

I told him that I "couldn't reveal my sources," but hinted that I knew someone who knew someone who worked in the bastard's office.

"What kinda name is that? *Prodski?* I bet it's Russian. I bet he's a Red. Or some kinda Jew. The fuckin' piece of shit. They almost killed me in that fuckin' place. Stuck all kinds of things in me. Hooked me up to machines. Shocked me in the head. Forced me to swallow all kinds of shit. They fuckin' tortured me. And they were all foreigners. Fuckin' Indians, Jews, Chinks. So this is the chief fuck. Prodski. A Red."

I asked him to calm down, because we didn't "want them to know that we knew." "This is our secret," I said. "You have to keep it to yourself. If they find out I told you, they'll come after me for sure. You know how they are. How rotten and mean they are. They'll send me to Courtland. That is, if they don't kill me first."

"The fucks!"

I handed him the sketch and told him to kept it safe and make absolutely sure that none of the staff saw it.

"Prodski," he said again, staring down at the paper with hateful, mad eyes as if the image had come to life for him. "I'm gonna get this fuck. Just as soon as I get out." He lowered his voice to a near whisper. "I got a couple of guns at home. The cops don't know about them. Nobody knows. I even learned how to make a bomb. Nobody knows about that either."

"Could come in handy," I said.

"Yeah," he said, smiling savagely.

"Remember, this is just between us." I told him that we'd talk more about it later, and that for now he should put that sketch away.

"Yeah, right," he said, folding up the paper. "Thanks, man. This is great. Fuckin' great."

Who would have thought months ago that I'd actually be looking forward to chatting with a bona fide maniac.

I SAT IN my room for a while, feeling quite sedate, quite satisfied. The windowpanes had darkened. Evening had arrived. And I'd made it through another day. And had made considerable progress as well.

I finally got up and went to the window. High-rises and tower blocks in the far distance were turning into silhouettes filled here and there by squares of yellow light. They looked unreal, theatrical. And so did the wisp of a cloud that was still visible in the deep blue sky and resembled a piece of stretched cotton.

I felt oddly stronger now and more at peace with myself than I'd ever felt in my life.

I walked to the dayroom where everyone was now gathered for supper. Mandy, who was among the living again, had saved the seat next to her—saved it for me. I was rather touched by the gesture and also glad that she'd managed to pull herself together again. She seemed to have celebrated her little recovery by exchanging the sad white hospital robe she'd worn earlier for a red silk dressing grown, which her sister or the family maid had probably brought her from home.

"Hey," she said, "you look different. I mean better. I'm used to seeing you in those crummy old clothes. Yeah, you look good, sort of casual. Neat, you know? Kind of yuppie."

"Too bad you didn't see me when I left. I was really dressed up then. Very stylish—if I must say so myself."

"Yeah, I'm sorry I missed it. I was feeling like shit for most of the day. But Wally told me about it. Said that you looked very classy. Like some millionaire character in some frigging movie—I forget which. Well, you know Wally . . . So how was your solo? Get any sex?" She laughed at this teasing question, which I ignored.

"Everything went well," I lied. "It was nice to be out. Perhaps a little tiring after a while. To be honest, I didn't mind so much about coming back. When all is said and done, this isn't such a bad place to rest."

"Maybe you'd like to rent a room," she said, rather amazed by my remark. "Jesus, give me a break."

"Oh—before I forget . . ." I reached into my pants pocket and took out the tube of Parisian Ruby Red.

She was so grateful that I'd remembered the lipstick that she gave me a little kiss on my cheek. Her lips were very soft and I wished they'd lingered a bit. "Thanks," she said, "I love this fucking shade. And it looks very sexy on me. I need a mirror. But I'll put it on later and show you."

We had chicken croquettes for dinner. Perhaps it was only because I'd eaten basically nothing all day, but the meal actually tasted rather decent for a change. In fact, I wouldn't have minded another potion if it had been available.

After dinner I joined Mandy on her favorite couch. We chatted on about this and that. I told her about my solo, mixing relatively true incidents with made-up tales. It was as if I were a writer combining fiction with nonfiction. And Mandy seemed to enjoy my accounts, both the real and the fake. I made sure that all of them were positive, cheerful—fun times in department stores, shops, galleries. I even threw in imaginary visits to the Central Park Zoo and Jennifer's French café. But as the time passed she began to yawn and briefly close her eyes and you could see that she was struggling to remain awake. Finally she gave in to her fatigue, curled up even more than she already had, curled up, in fact, right beside me, and rested her head on my shoulder. She must have felt very comfortable and secure in this position because she soon fell asleep. I didn't mind her head at all—her short hair was surprisingly smooth.

So I sat there quietly, almost motionless, trying not to disrupt Mandy's sleep. And as the television blared and Wally laughed and clapped, and as Mrs. Schulman stared out the window at the night sky, and Carl gloomily sipped coffee, and Maria mumbled angrily to herself, and Mrs. Clark knitted a scarf, and the nurses chatted in the nurses' station, and as a new patient, a new arrival, banged on the door of the Quiet Room and cried out in anguish, and as I looked down at Mandy snuggling against me, a thought crossed my mind that made me very happy and also very scared: I was home.